PT
2673      Muschg, Adolf, 1934-
.U78          The blue man and other stories /
A23       Adolf Muschg ; translated from the
1985      German by Marlis Zeller Cambon &
          Michael Hamburger. -- 1st ed. -- New
          York : G. Braziller, 1985.
              141 p. ; 22 cm.
          Contents: The scythe hand, or, The homestead
      -- The blue man -- Reparations, or, Making
      good -- Brami's view -- Grandfather's little
      pleasure -- Dinnertime -- The country house,
      or, Defaulted presence.
          ISBN 0-8076-1100-X

          1. Muschg, Adolf, 1934- --Translations into
      English. I. Title.

      PT2673.U78A23 1985          833'.914    [F]

                      WaOE              84-24439//r91

# THE BLUE MAN

TRANSLATED FROM THE GERMAN
BY MARLIS ZELLER CAMBON &
MICHAEL HAMBURGER

# THE BLUE MAN

---

## AND OTHER STORIES

## ADOLF MUSCHG

GEORGE BRAZILLER • NEW YORK

Published in the United States in 1985
by George Braziller, Inc.
Parts of this book appeared in slightly different form in the volume
*The Blue Man & Other Stories*, published in England in 1983 by
Carcanet New Press Ltd., 210 Corn Exchange Building, Manchester
M4 3BQ.
Acknowledgement is due to the following periodicals in which some
of the translations in this volume have appeared: *Encounter* 1975
for "The Scythe Hand or The Homestead": *Canto I*, 3, 1977 for
"Blue Man": *Canto II*, 1, 1978 for "Reparations or Making
Good;" and *Fiction VI*, 1, 1978 for "Brami's View."

LIBRARY OF CONGRESS CATALOGING IN PUBLICATION DATA

Muschg, Adolf, 1934–
The blue man & other stories.

Contents: The scythe man, or, The homestead—Blue
man—Reparations, or, Making Good—[etc.]
1. Muschg, Adolf, 1934–    —Translations, English.
I. Title.    II. Title: Blue man and other stories.
PT2673.U78A23  1985    833'.914    84–24439
ISBN 0–8076–1100–X

Designed by Joe Marc Freedman

Printed in the United States of America
First edition

# CONTENTS

# TRANSLATOR'S NOTE

Publishing a selection of Adolf Muschg's short stories begins to fill a significant gap in the availability of German language fiction in English translation. The current volume represents only a fraction of Muschg's prose. While his literary output is impressive in scope as well as volume—it ranges from plays, several novels, collections of short stories to literary criticism and poetics, a biography of his fellow resident of Zürich, Gottfried Keller—it is his short fiction, notably the volume *Liebesgeschichten* (Love Stories) which has found its way into translation: first into French (*Histoires d'amour*, 1975, in Philippe Jaccottet's version), then into English with Michael Hamburger's translation of one of the stories from that volume in 1975, *The Scythe Hand*, reprinted in this volume. My translations of several other stories appeared subsequently in the United States, and thanks are due to the editors of *CANTO*, Review of the Arts, for pioneering Muschg's work and for kindling my interest in this writer who should not be missing from the list of the best authors writing in German today. Like his older Swiss contemporaries, Max Frisch and Friedrich Dürrenmatt (both, however, well represented in English translation), Muschg incorporates in his writing what have come to be called Swiss themes: the tension between the unique political and cultural structure which is Switzerland and the larger German speaking world of its neighbors; the dilemma arising from this situation: belonging to that context and breaking out of its confines; defensiveness and rejection, and the ongoing dialogue over the Swiss self-image which has been in crisis for the past decades, no doubt as a result of shock waves from the Second World War. But Muschg's "Swissness" is only one facet of the complexity of this writer; in most cases, certainly in our selection of short stories, it provides nothing more than a local flavor to themes that must be considered universally relevant, for they reflect existential modes which cannot be limited to one national background. Muschg is above all a German-speaking European and shares in the themes of twentieth-century Europe: existential anxiety, metaphysical skepticism, distrust in human institutions, a strong psychological interest in the motivating forces of our conscious and unconscious selves, and of course the dilemma of language between renewal and limits of communication.

All of Muschg's characters are men without qualities, ordinary people with extraordinary anguish. *Love Stories* is the title of his first collection of short stories, and it ought to be the subtitle of all his later volumes, notably those of short fiction, because they all deal with love for a misbegotten and warped mankind, man in his lonely sensibility, craving shelter, pretending fulfillment in the embrace of another equally incarcerated human being. Nothing can bridge the gulf between the voids; there is no awakening from the private nightmares. All of us, Muschg seems to say, lead lives of quiet desperation; what matters is only the degree of alienation tolerable in our everyday existence.

Muschg the narrator remains always present. As he bores into his people's minds, dissecting layer after layer of their consciousness, describing their inner world in terms of an outer one, he does so with an almost obsessive attention to detail, registering like a seismograph the most minute fluctuations of a mood and its projections into a landscape, an object, a gesture. Muschg is a master of the miniature scene, and it is therefore in the small form, in the short story, that he creates his most haunting sceneries—landscapes of the mind cast into expressionist images of our outer reality and pastoral scenes filled with the flora of his native country.

The range of Muschg's narrative voice is impressive: there is the halting voice of a mountain peasant who in the antiquated rhetorical flourishes of another world grafted upon his alpine dialect, pleads for a court's understanding of his life's circumstances. His language accentuates the gulf between the moral codes of a respectable society and the creature needs of a humanity on the fringe. And at the other end of the range stands the sarcastic portrait of an emotional cripple, victimized by circumstances, victimizer behind the facade of middleclass propriety. The deceptively light tone, the flippancy with which this everyman's climb to bourgeois respectability is told, emphasizes the reader's uneasy awareness of an emotional quagmire and its threatening implications: Hanna Arendt's thoughts on the banality of evil come to mind. There are a great many elegiac landscape descriptions, evoking nostalgia for lost childhoods but also holding out the promise of shelter and belonging. Nowhere are Muschg's people—his mouthpiece

*9*

is almost always a male figure—farther removed from that promise and closer to despair and self-annihilation than in the contemplation of a nature scene; Muschg, in many ways a late Romantic, writes some of his most gripping pages when he pits man against an impassive and hauntingly beautiful landscape.

His style, then, ranges from the lofty to the colloquial, always in close proximity to each other, with an occasional Swiss-German echo; the predominant characteristic of his style, however, is a highly literary tone sustained through mimetic speech in the third person, as the imaged self registers its own feelings and constantly takes its spiritual pulse.

This lofty and often lyrical prose, need it be said, presents itself as a linguistic challenge to the translator, as a forbidding and unassailable structure of elliptical syntax, Chinese box metaphors, lexical innovations which, given the particular structure of German, can be absorbed in that language, but render translation all the more difficult. The ambiguities both in grammar and in reference are many and always deliberate. Questions and inversions are part of this style, suggesting a sense of availability, of approximation rather than certainty. It is a nervously vibrating language, circling its object in now narrowing, now widening gyres, restlessly searching for the right word, the always more incisive image to arrest an elusive essence.

I have resisted the temptation (and many suggestions) to tone down Muschg's high style, to render his intricate prose into "smooth" English. If Muschg can be compared to any writer in the English language, it is William Faulkner, whose highly literary and at times precious prose, tempered with the vernacular in a Southern lilt, all but exhausts the tolerance for a self-reflective, introverted

English style. With his syntactic convolutions, abundant participial structures, long-winded sentences weaving together thought processes and simultaneous action, Muschg is closer to this great American writer than to any other author. In one aspect only have I followed the recommendation to smooth out Muschg's style: the Helvetic timbre in occasional semantic and syntactic usage had to be sacrificed in the translation, unless such expressions were an integral part of the narration. In such cases I have tried to approximate.

While translation to some extent is an act of violation in the effort to preserve the integrity of the host language, I have opted for the opposite approach, preferring to strain the tolerance of English in order to convey the edge of Muschg's intensely personal style; by pushing language to the brink he accentuates a sense of agony over the human condition and draws the reader into an open-ended quest.

MARLIS ZELLER CAMBON
*Connecticut College*

# THE
# BLUE
# MAN

# THE
# SCYTHE HAND
## OR
# THE HOMESTEAD

Perhaps the Court of Enquiry is not aware that with my
late wife Elisabeth I farmed for fifteen years at Frogs' Well
and was of good repute there, had enough to live on, too,
till the same burned to the ground for dubious reasons in
the year 1951 with our son Christian, aged two at that
time, and I also lost all our livestock, as well as vehicles,
because the fire spread too fast and the fire brigade did not
arrive in time. Frogs' Well had been in the family for more
than a century, and my grandfather farmed it to everyone's satisfaction in his time. Consequently my father,
deceased, was even elected to the School Board, and I take
the liberty of mentioning that I was able to attend the
Secondary School at Krummbach, because my mother,
deceased, skimped no sacrifice. Water could have been
drawn from the hydrant by the well, but the fire chief
insisted on his view that this was frozen over, which was
quite correct, but all that was needed was to break the thin

ice. So more than one hour passed before the hose was laid across from Hasenrain, and the main building too could not be saved. The death of Christian gave rise to many ugly rumors, although he was quite small and we had always looked after him well. That was a great blow to us at the time. Since the indemnity was never adequate and at first we were housed at Shady Bank, that too gave rise to sharp friction, and my dear wife survived it only for one year, because she had caught cold during the conflagration, which turned out to be cancer. That also is a cause of great distress to us, when everyone knew that we used to manage well and had been punished enough as it was, and had paid our gound-rent regularly. But the indemnity was reduced out of malice, and the operation cost 5000 francs, which I could hardly raise, and it became too much for the farmeress at Shady Bank, because of my daughters, although Lina was already 22 and gave a hand everywhere, as I did in the field, while they said that I scared the cows and therefore must not milk them. It wasn't Barbara's fault that she was only three years old, though she did cause a lot of work in which as a man I could not assist enough, and the farmeress at Shady Bank was herself expecting. So we had to move out and take out a lease for Torgel Alp from the municipality, for which I had reason to be grateful too, because the previous tenant had caught his death there after running down the farm and hanging himself. The place was too lonely for him as well.

So up on Torgel Alp nothing had been done for years, but Lina and I got the homestead back into working order, and we succeeded, too, in bringing up Barbara satisfactorily, so that she kept her health. Only her way to school was so long that in winter she could not always manage it, so that she fell behind and lost much joy, even though I cleared the track each morning and this wasn't even laid down in the contract.

I cleared the road as far as the dairy farm, but didn't hang about there, nor in the village, because of the people, not even to collect money owing for milk. If that gave rise to new rumors, that's typical, but the real trouble was the great remoteness of the homestead, which often set in as early as mid-October because of snow.

Also, I had to go over completely to dairy farming, which I should not have dreamed of doing at Frogs' Well, but carried out in the teeth of all sorts of obstacles.

Also, the ground-rent was so high that with the best will in the world we had to borrow again. At first I had the good luck to be able to graze 15-20 bullocks, privately, but then for no evident reason the number decreased, although I only asked for my due, the bullocks returned to the valley in good condition, too, but I never stayed there long enough to forestall the rumors. Furthermore, my older daughter Lina was often sick, which did not affect the running of the farm, since I kept her at her work and exertions all the same, and our younger one had had to learn early on to help her sister, even though this kept her away from school. I must add that Lina was a strong support for me without words and despite the pain she had in her belly, and would be still if she hadn't been taken into care now, for which she is not to blame, and I only hope that now she is receiving medical attention, because she has earned it. It was a blow to us when the municipality would send no more bullocks for grazing because of irreg-ularities that were completely unfounded, or that were due only to all the special circumstances there, and because I didn't spend all my time defending myself, so that I was thrown back on my meager resources.

Sheer slander it was, their saying that I was out of my mind, only because I could no longer control a twitching in my cheek, and I'm sure that caused no inconvenience to anyone, but never allowed a bad word to cross my lips, as the Vicar can testify, as long as he came to see us, that is, for he stopped, as everyone knows, until it was too late. When people wouldn't look at me because of the twitch, I sent Barbara out with the milk, which would have done her no harm, I'm sure, and she only bought the most necessary things at the shop, because we couldn't afford more in any case, and if she sometimes stayed for a while it was only because she had to wait and other people can afford more than they could in my time.

And if they say my milk wasn't 100%, no one has proved that and none of those gentlemen saw how I looked after my cattle, they always got fed before we did, and as for sick cows, I had to telephone to report such a case if it occurred, so that the vet could get there in time, even though a jeep was put in his disposal by the municipality.

I too am a member of the municipality, but that doesn't mean that my daughters can simply be taken into care, only because they aren't to blame for anything. It is always being said, too, that I ceased to go to church or to confession, but there I should like you to consider that I should have gone when the trouble started, but it was too far away, and so we had to cope with the trouble on our own. If that is sin, my daughters couldn't help it, and you gentlemen of the Court should admit it, because of their youth for one thing, because of their poverty for another, and you should take into account that, given all those things, Barbara may have been a bit backward. Nevertheless, when it had happened, no sort of deterioration took place in the household, no, it improved if anything, since at last we lived together in peace and could raise the ground-rent for once, which was like a miracle, and I thanked God for it, until the Vicar arrived and, after him, the Justice of the Peace, all because of the slander. For it is my opinion that if you leave a family alone for so long you must allow them to solve their problems in their own way. But since she has been taken into care now, I don't want to stand in the way of my daughter's happiness, only hope that this is what's in question, not somebody's profit because my daughter has learned how to work, and I also request that there shall be no recriminations, because I did not corrupt her, although, as you know, unlawful acts did take place. These were only for the sake of her peace, as Barbara can confirm if she likes, and I forgive her in my heart, she must not fret because she got me into prison, for that was our fate, it seems, and that's all there is to it. So I will thank God that she came down from Torgel Alp, and beg the honorable Court only for some attention to her, so that she survives. I was fond of her, there's no getting away from it, and consequently could not do otherwise, and wouldn't know today what to do. And even my late wife would have had no objection, I know that, when I had the privilege to know her kind heart for twenty-four years, and she was glad, too, to be blessed with late children, first Barbara, then Christian who stayed behind in the fire. That is why, too, she departed this life and left the family to their own devices, that was a bit much all at once, when on top of it you are penalized and have to move to Torgel Alp. If my older daughter Lina hadn't taken after her late mother, hadn't been the split image of her, I don't know what would have become of us up there.

One should not forget, though, that a girl has other thoughts in her head beyond housekeeping, even an older girl.

In any case Lina was no longer ill when you separated

us, that may not have suited the Rev. Vicar, because his mind boggled, but then he was clerical and past the age when a person is tormented.

But should Lina now be ailing once more, then it's those people who did that to her, for my daughter has a strong constitution and recovers every time she is needed. I myself couldn't know — could I? — that at 57 I should be tormented again, and it was a cold morning too. I was about to go out and feed the cows, and I noticed that she hadn't lit the fire, but the kitchen was empty, and your breath froze in front of your nose. I was startled, dear Court of Enquiry, for I can only say that nothing like that had happened in ten years, even when she did have a bellyache she'd drag herself downstairs and put the coffee on the stove. All the windows were covered in frost, and the place quiet as a churchyard, that's where she ought to have appeared to me, for it hadn't been as quiet as that since the death of my wife. But this didn't occur to me at that instant, I can promise you, didn't come over me till later.

Went upstairs to the bedroom, the little one was asleep for we'd always let her sleep when it was too cold, and there was only a little boxroom for her, but a warm bed, there she was coziest, why take her anywhere else. My only thought was that there could be one fewer of us again, and that made me shake with fear, I never so much as knocked on Lina's door but tore it open. I only write this much so that you will know the circumstances, not so that you'll come to dirty conclusions again. For there in the cold bedroom my wife sat in her shift, her bare shift, honorable Court of Enquiry, never turned her head but went on as before, leaning forward a little, so as to see herself in the mirror, only a small one it was, and passed the brush over her hair. But she did that so slowly that this slowness, together with the mere shift and the breath clouding the mirror, so that she had to wipe it clear with her free hand, all this cut into my heart and made me feel quite faint, I can't describe it, when my wife had been dead all those years. What are you doing, I asked, why don't you stop, or you'll catch cold. She said, without turning round: Why not, she said, quite calm and funny. Later she said she had dreamed of her mother, and only then, I promise you, I remembered that I too had dreamed of her mother, but by then it was too late.

As long as I stood there, by the door, I saw only that she didn't so much as turn round and, in consequence, that her hair had already turned gray in places. You should bear in mind that Lina was not quite 37, which is normal, save that as her father I had never paid attention to it, also the cold, and that the shock had left me in an abnormal state of mind. That is why everything happened so fast that I can't recall how it came about, I didn't lie about that, even though you want to know the exact details, but what's the use of them now. On my honor and salvation, all I know is that suddenly I felt relieved and Lina's face, with a rosy and languid look she hadn't had since her childhood, lay beside me on the pillow, and the two of us breathed. I am sorry I cannot tell you more, save that it happened, and that was all, and you are grown-up people after all, nor was I aware of the illegality of the act at that moment, but it wasn't my age, on the contrary, 57 doesn't amount to old age, I wish it did. Next item, I went to feed the animals, and when I returned Lina was at the stove as usual, humming a tune, and the coffee was already made. That's how it went till the evening, save that I couldn't get to sleep and was cruelly tormented. I drank several glasses of brandy, fill yourself up, I said to myself, and you won't feel so sore about it. But this was not the case, the whole mood of the place was changed, too, like at Christmas, for which reason I retired for self-abuse, as in all the previous years, when tormented. The mood would not leave me, though, but you must not think that this happened often, I'd been tormented daily only in the four or five years after my wife's death, then once a month perhaps, and then it stopped completely and I lived like a decent widower. I said to myself, what's up, then, you have no right to any Christmas any more, have you, you aren't even sleepy, and so I took a walk over to the cattle, which nearly always helped.

Although by then I had only two cows of my own and six goats, and your breath froze on your nose, I got into a sweat as soon as I so much as looked at them, though I'd seen the same thing a thousand times if I'd seen it once, and they turned their heads to look at me, too, as though they wanted to do something to me, as though bewitched, so that I went out again and on and on through the snow, as far as the place where I took it into my head to lie down, thinking that will make you feel better. But then in the cold it struck me that my daughters wouldn't be able to raise the money for my funeral, but would be exposed to mockery, though behind hands held to the face as usual, I didn't want them to suffer that, couldn't get my daughters out of my mind at all, but not in the way you think, and I got up again. So I suddenly found myself back at the homestead, must have walked in a semi-circle, that happens in the snow. It wasn't my own homestead either, I'd always known that, but when you're tired and the above has occurred, you see things as though for the first time. So I stood like a stranger in front of this homestead and no longer knew what was what, was afraid to go in. I thought, something will happen of itself if you stand here long enough, sooner or later the music will stop, for I had heard music all that night, and the stars were out, it was getting colder fast, near dawn. But because the snow itself made everything bright I saw that a window upstairs was open, please, my God, don't, I said to that, but nothing helped, so I called out, shut it, then, shut it, you pig, yes, that's what I called out, but don't know whether she heard me, my voice was feeble too, and all remained as it was.

If I turned my head a bit could see it more clearly, but still, couldn't tell for certain, what, if I looked at it straight it was there at one moment, gone the next, but it was something white all the time.

A man wants to know, gentlemen, whether someone his own is standing so long at an open window in such a frost and catching her death of it, so I went inside and upstairs, but it wasn't the torment, when I couldn't even feel my own feet. In Lina's bedroom everything was open, and the window too, but no one was standing there, and I began to fear what she might have done to herself. Stretched out my hand, I did, to where it was darkest, for that's where the bed was, till I felt something warm, something alive, that was there. Said, Thank God for that, without her being able to hear me, because she was under the cover and I wanted to comfort her. But she held on to my hand and said, come on, then, you idiot, you chicken, and said it quite clearly, and I responded to it, because I suddenly lost all consciousness of myself, and it must have happened for the second time, for suddenly there was peace again and no music any more. You must not hold that chicken against my daughter, it was clearly meant to be a sort of joke. I had called out pig, too, and hadn't meant it. You can call that sin, but there was this cold all the time, and I'm no chicken I'm sorry to say, so I stayed till it was warm. No one thanks you, anway, for suffering the cold, and the need is too great to be forgiven us, as the Vicar said, whether we live as husband and wife now or not.

After that Lina was cured of her bellyache, we were kinder to each other, too, and took good care of each other, and that year I could pay off my ground-rent in time, because a blessing had been put on it. Was able to buy two more cows and have all four served, and they produced cow calves and got a prize a year later, which was made possible because the judges at Krummbach didn't know so much about my situation, and it became evident that without prejudice I could manage well, received a loan from the Small Farmers' Assistance too, which enabled me to have the roof re-thatched and to build a long-needed reservoir, but created more bad blood in the village. For, High Court of Justice, it is true, on my oath, that one can stand on one's head, bad blood can't be made any better, especially if the village is small.

It was also true that I could have a new dress bought for each of my daughters, which nowadays is no luxury even in remote places, and I waited till the sales for that and certainly did not live in splendor and affluence. When we only had just enough for us to get used to our state of affairs.

As for me, I can only add that since the death of my lamented wife I had never lived in a family, but this was now the case more than ever. My younger daughter caught me singing, too, as I whitewashed the cowshed. That was more than I deserved, I'm sure, and I give all the credit for it to my dear daughters.

After finishing her school years Barbara did not want to take any employment, since she'd had enough teasing, the spasms in her face grew more violent too, which she must have inherited, though in myself I was not always aware of them. The vet couldn't find a good reason for them either, save that they were nervous, though I should have paid him to the last penny for his pills. So it came about that Barbara stayed with us, nor expressed any desire for an apprenticeship, which I should certainly have let her have, never wanting to deprive my daughters of any-thing, since I am fond of them both, though not in the way you think. Nor did I know that in the shed she was subject to regular molestation by the scythe hand, that Füllemann who is well known to you, who took advantage of her extremity, because she never said anything about it in public, perhaps thinking we had enough trouble already. It would have been better if she had, though, for in that case I should have bashed in the scythe hand's skull without qualms. What I am charged with, though, because the scythe hand got it out of her, that was quite different from the gossip it gave rise to, the reason why I am now in prison. Because I was fond of my daughter, and concerned about her health, about which I knew no better when even a vet wouldn't take the trouble, I couldn't resist, but I never implanted any pride in her on that score, so that she would go and boast to the scythe hand about something that certainly happened as an emergency measure and under the stress of too much molestation, when she was still half a child, as she is to this day.

For, High Court of Justice, you wouldn't have done any different either if your daughter had begged for it so urgently and you couldn't bear to see her suffer, only because the girl doesn't know the facts of life, but was physically mature and plagued by it, again because of the remoteness of the homestead, which could happen only up on Torgel Alp. Our Frogs' Well was burnt down, as you know, my wife departed and I alone with the girls, of whom one was now 37, the other 21, a great gap, but not with regard to the female body, that makes it hard to show no love when Lina is better all at once, but the younger one sleeps just behind the thin partition and is tormented in her fashion.

Since she slept lightly I wanted to relieve her of that, there was no other motive, and the longer it went on the less anyone thought anything of it, if the scythe hand hadn't got it out of her, I bet he had his reasons. And if it is said that she burst into tears, I'd like to have seen you if as half a child still you'd got under the scythe hand, and that wasn't till seven months later, the tears too came because of the Vicar, who got there late enough, it had never happened with me.

Rather the facts of the case were as follows, my younger daughter came to me in the spring, complaining that I didn't esteem her, because Lina was privileged, and she was only her sister. At first I dismissed that, till my younger girl went to bed ill and wouldn't get up again, the twitches in her face got so bad, too, that mine broke out again and I feared for her sanity, and she sang so loud when I was with Lina that I thought a sow was being struck, but she never dared come in, because she was a decent girl. In March, though, she developed such a belly-ache that I thought, Oh, hell, maybe it would be better for you to give her peace, talked about it with Lina, who'd turned into a real housewife. But it isn't true that she advised me to do it, she only knew, what must be, must be. So, when Lina had gone to the road house with the milk, I took Barbara a jug of milk warm from the cow to her bedroom, since I had to take everything up to her, which became troublesome, and it was March 23rd. She grabbed hold of my hand at once so that I could feel if there wasn't a swelling there, and when I felt her she started that cruel screaming again, as well as spasms which ran visibly across her whole body, and I felt so sorry for her that I couldn't help myself but allowed what followed to occur. Then she got up quite amiable and smiled like a rogue, but I was too fond of my daughter to bear her any grudge, only begged her sincerely never to let it happen again. Whereupon she quite easily drank the milk which she had pushed far away from her before, and went quite sensibly to the kitchen, and prepared an evening meal, which she hadn't done for a long time, indeed started cooking and frying so much that I got alarmed and we fed well that evening, in great obliviousness even drank brandy till it gave rise to new acts, and I was even the instigator, which I would beg to have taken into account today in my daughters' favor. That was March 23rd. For I must add that because of constant physical labor I am still full of sap, quite unexpectedly, nor knew any remedy for it till Lina took the matter into her hand, but this occurred with good will on both sides, like the relations with my younger daughter, which I did not need any more, as you will understand.

But let the respected Court tell me of a way to help a poor person like Barbara out of her predicament, when the partition is thin and there's no prospect of her finding a suitable man, when already at school she couldn't keep up, but only because of Torgel Alp, where one couldn't make a secret of our situation, as other people do. For, dear Court, poverty had come first, I must say that quite plainly, and poverty brings many troubles in its train, of which one can relieve only the most pressing, if no one else offers any help.

It would have been the first time I preferred one daughter to the other, that is why I had to take her on in turn, not because I was tormented. After that all went smoothly in our house, you can ask anyone, and if it was a sin and no one wants to have anything to do with us now, I do beseech you not to make too great an issue of our intercourse, for neither did we, but peace was the main thing, and we did not disturb anyone, but were never bedded on roses. And I assure you that the abomination was no unmitigated pleasure, a thing that is quite unknown on Torgel Alp, but only a kind of comfort.

Earlier on we did have a conscience about it, but that ceased because my daughters no longer suffered from a bellyache, and this was better than a deal of worrying about it and even made us quite merry at times in the winter. There are always people who talk about their conscience but don't tell a man all the same what's to be done against the cold or against pains, at least nobody told us. When the Vicar arrived at last we no longer expected him and didn't really know what to do about it, and nor did he. For he walked up quite slowly, Lina saw him from a long way off, and she said, O my God. So, when he could think of nothing to say but only asked, don't you want to confess, I could not back him up and answered quite legitimately, I wouldn't know what to confess, and he replied, he thought I did know, and he couldn't even look me straight in the eyes. For years he could have observed how Barbara's face twitched, and my daughter Lina's bellyache, but all that had been nothing to him, not so now that all was going well, though without his blessing. I told him what I thought about that. He said that he never listened to gossip but was answerable for preventing the spreading of the bacillus, which would make half the community sick at the very mention of us, and that I could bear even less to be answerable for it, either toward God or toward my daughters. I said I could bear to be answerable for many things as long as a man needs help and the ways are not always clear to him, in short I refused point-blank to make a confession of it, when he still couldn't look me in the face, but only stroked his hip with one hand.

I then offered him a glass of schnapps, whereupon he did not come in, but said: if you will not avail yourself of the secrecy of confession I must ask you as a fellow citizen to give yourself up, because otherwise you will be in trouble, you will make the village unhappy with your state of affairs, or would you prefer to have your roof set on fire one night? High Court of Justice, that gave me a fright, to hear him talk of a fire, when I had lost one child in a fire before, and there too the cause had remained obscure, although I had never given offense to anyone. Whereupon my daughter Barbara rushed into the room and made our distress very great by screaming that the Vicar was a dirty old man and ought to wipe his nose after sticking it into everyone's pots, when it wasn't his business, and did the scythe hand confess too what he had done to her? So the cat was out of the bag, as far as the scythe hand was concerned, and it then came out that the same had repeatedly lain in wait for her when she was helpless because of the heavy pails she was carrying, and had grabbed hold of her in spite of her protests. Finally, at the end of June, he had gone so far as to bash her head against a stone near the milking-shed, so that she couldn't struggle, and used her, because there was no help for her nearby, and on top of that had said to her mockingly, how well the meadow had been mown already, and hadn't he hurt her? Whereupon my daughter had screamed in her half-conscious state, with his miserable stub he couldn't do anyone any harm, let alone any good. Whereupon the same had merely buttoned up his trousers, saying, all right, all the more power to our buck, who had all the nanny-goats to himself, now that the farmer had come to an agreement with his daughters, and she was to give his regards to the whole happy household, put on his hat and left. That was a sad speech, since it is well known that lonely men have to make do with animals, when for years they cannot find a single human being, something I did not do even in my worst plight, but only deviated from the straight and narrow path to give my daughters peace, of which certainly the younger one ought not to have bragged, nor did I ever implant such arrogance in her heart.

Nevertheless, High Court of Justice, you should take into account that she was used by the scythe hand, and this without any understanding between them.

I have always believed that in such things there must be an agreement, and that two are needed for that, even with poor folk, and a little joy, which even beasts do not fail to feel in their fashion. But between my daughters and me this was so, because we did it for the sake of warmth and it was not the most important thing, but so that the family would be kept together, nor was violence ever used. But the scythe hand confessed his crime to the Vicar and got rid of his sin by bringing down justice upon our homestead, and we all had to pay dearly for Barbara's little lapse into pride. Now you want to know more than I can offer you, when the real shock and perdition came only after everyone took such a lively interest in the affair.

The scythe hand got off lightly because he is young and daft as a duck, but older flesh is never forgiven when it's tormented, and yet its trials are harder than those of any loud-mouthed young ruffian. But if my daughter Lina had been younger, and without my fears, I should never have violated her, but it was because I saw her gray hairs and pity took hold of me like a rage that this daughter of mine was not to be taken for what she was, but must drag her bellyache around in silence all her life, which to this day seems more bestial to me than everything else. And this too was not because of the flesh, but because the flesh is tormented by a soul and has nothing left to hope for if it finds no warmth, something I could not bear to watch any longer. Everything else, as I have set it down, followed logically from that, because I could not slight Barbara, and never pursued those relations for their own sake, but only so that the girls should have some kindness in thir lives. And I raise no objection now if the whole responsibility falls on me, because men should always know better. I did not know better, only did what I could in those criminal acts to find the right course.

By taking my daughters into care and appointing a guardian doubtless you know better, and I only ask that my daughters, because they are girls, will be spared as much of the disgrace as possible, perhaps in another valley, where they are not known. For we have never in our lives received as much attention as after the Vicar's visit, in which connection I will name only the Justice of the Peace, then Lina's old teacher, twice the constable, and then a regular police action even with dogs, as though we had ever thought of running away, when we couldn't even have known where to. All the nets are so tightly meshed everywhere. I have never seen my daughters again since then, and enough of cross-examinations, if I may say so, don't know whether they had to undergo them too and if that was of any use, they will hardly have understood your words, but surely taken them to heart. So let me apologize at this point on their behalf. Nor do I want or receive a letter ever again from my daughters, if that could do them harm, would only like to know whether they are well cared for as far as the circumstances permit, and should be much gratified to obtain an assurance to that effect from you. I also beg for instructions as to how, once and for all, I am to express myself under interrogation, since I can see very well that I was far from satisfying the gentlemen with my way of speaking, but may well have made matters even worse, though I spoke the truth.

About the abnormality in my face which I got rid of but which has now returned, I beg of you not to be disturbed, nor to be put off by it, if that is possible. I shall manage all right.

Details of the criminal act, I am sorry to say, embarrass me, since the process is familiar enough to grown-up people, and I should only like to observe that most of those can go through the same in more favorable circumstances, nor do I believe that more is to be learned about it from my daughters than what every real man or woman knows.

Make an end of it, at last, honorable Court, because you are better off, or I could begin to say things I should be sorry about, all right, I will admit to having led my daughters into misdemeanor, if you insist on it and I can lessen the plight of those girls by saying so.

Perhaps it is possible, too, to choose a guardian for my daughters who is not a clergyman. These, I regret to say, often fall into false assumptions which their wards then have to swallow, but can't always, which leads to tragedies.

Every man and woman is tormented in their way, and I have learned that those who are stronger will then oppress others because of it, by which I don't mean to deny their good will, and please don't hold those words against me.

I have written to you only because my spoken words are not adequate for your satisfaction and because perhaps you will take the opportunity, nonetheless, to convey a greeting to my daughters, which I set down herewith, but this too not for my sake, but because in those years my daughters grew accustomed again to a little warmth.

May it please you to tell them that they are on my mind by day and by night, but not in the way the High Court of Justice thinks.

# THE
# BLUE
# MAN

I am not stingy. It is only that I am afraid to spend money.
To put it more precisely: I am afraid of money altogether,
afraid of its unpredictable behavior toward those who have
to live frugally and have to be concerned about it. As a
child I experienced that power of money so vividly at
home, as if it had been part of the air I was breathing, or a
slight persistent chest pain one did not have to take too
seriously, as long as it didn't become stronger. Both my
parents worked, but without their having to tell me I knew
that the money they earned barely sufficed for our liveli-
hood. We children grew up near some orchards in a community that was still rural, and there were always apples on
the ground for us; but what filled us with anxiety was that
the total and relentless effort of both parents was obviously
required to keep want from pressing at our four walls—
which, in my dreams, were already beginning to bend. All
it would take was for my mother to break an ankle one

day—and how fragile her ankles seemed!—and then something would give way: and I believed I knew there would be no stopping it, and whatever little brightness surrounded my childhood would be wiped away in one terrible sweep, of a kind I could not imagine. Between us and disaster there was only money, but I felt that those few hundred monthly francs, by making themselves available with such disdainful parsimony, were secretly in league with disaster, an evil mockery which did not deserve my parents' drudgery but left them no other choice.

How different life was in the homes of some of my friends! There you were obviously on an equal footing with money, indeed, there was never any need to mention it. It had become tractable, tame, it had settled with my friend Hugo's mother into one corner of the sofa and chatted so amiably through her lips, as if I might still be rescued and were not the son of her cleaning woman. It promised something it never had at our house—security, yes, security against death. Children have a fine sense of how narrow the cloth is from which their coats are cut. They get used to making no unnecessary move that would give them away to gloom, that eternally young cat: some—thing is still moving there, pounce upon it. I forced myself into a cautious lifestyle because early on I was conscious of how I must have provoked a frivolous fate—walking about as I did, lankily, with hunched up shoulders, incapable of any sense of humor to confront it with. I knew it so well, because I had readily joined others in the tormenting of a schoolfriend who physically fit this description too. And if I shied away from their most extreme cruelties, not daring to do to him what I myself was afraid of, it was only because I was even more afraid of becoming conspicuous, of attracting the attention of that force I saw glimmering in the eyes of the ringleaders. It came as no surprise to me

when that schoolfriend—Bruno was his name—drowned
one day in the lake, although, as everyone pointed out, he
knew how to swim. I knew very well how long the irra-
tional element must have waited to devour him and how it
was already twitching in our fingers, as they tightened
around Bruno's neck. Poverty, as it was written into
Bruno's pale, mawkish face, was a terrible lure for his
death. Since his mother, like mine, cleaned staircases for
other people, I firmly believed that he had drowned in my
place and nothing would harm me anymore.

I settled into life, without causing any uproars, and like
my siblings went to Middle School. Despite my good grades
I dared not advance farther. The step into the *Kantons-*
*schule* which my teacher encouraged (did not something
flash behind his glasses? I knew what it was, it could not
trick me), I could have taken only with my eyes closed,
and this would have been precisely the right moment my
good luck was waiting for to let go of me forever. To be
sure, I did not feel altogether safe among so many other
young apprentices, but somewhat better camouflaged.
Whatever there was that wanted to seize me in its clutches
could now easily seize someone else by mistake, as it had
done in the case of Bruno. So I ran neither ahead nor at
the end of the field, but saw to it that I remained a
tolerated part of the pack and an elusive target.

Irony, to be sure, which spins the web of all relation-
ships, somehow got me, perhaps because of my anxious
scruples—into the career of an accountant, therefore into
immediate, even overwhelming, closeness to money. But
in precisely this way I seemed to have outsmarted it, in the
same way a bullfighter (I saw a bullfight on my last
vacation; I shall talk about it later on) presses himself
without risk against the side of the monstrous beast once its
horns are past him. This murderous angle, calculated with

accuracy, was also the safest. Money simply had to spare me; working quietly at my desk I even relished the illusion of dominance. Without a touch it allowed me to arrange it in columns whose dizzying numbers did not affect me personally. It played along, pretending to balance without remainder under my hand; and if I had to live off the shreds of such magnanimous play, I still considered it enough for myself. I had prudently secured my affairs early in life. When my parents died—something they had always threatened to do, sometimes by words, more often by their silent weariness—we children were already safe, each of us was earning an income. The vortex that forms around a grave and that had already sucked everything reliable from my childhood could no longer devour us.

The fact that I granted myself a vacation in a Mediter-ranean country this year may lead to the conclusion either that I had shaken off my doom or that it had lost interest in me. It would have been wonderful. But I moved too early. I let myself be lured into the sun, forgetting the shadow I cast, a shadow oblivious to my feeling secure and which took the shape of the blue man. Indeed, I had so improved my situation that I lost my memory, my fear, which remains my only hope and which might have been my salvation.

It all started out so well. I loved my wife; if such words suited me, I would say: I am still in love with her. My wife brought a small fortune into our marriage which, thanks to my connections in the bank, I was able to invest very well. When my wife was expecting I considered it imperative to take out life insurance. We often teased each other about the amount—then I thought she enjoyed the game, now I am not so sure anymore. At the time I felt that I had gained an immense freedom, which I gladly paid for, with part of my salary. It went so far that I even dared joke about the insurance, this strange contract with the future against its own uncertainty. What is it then that we fear more than our own death? What is it that we feel the need to protect ourselves against, beyond the grave? Strange as this may sound, in my case it was still the specter of poverty, the fear of being exposed to heaven knows what kind of want and deprivation, a fear which is obviously made to outlast me. That my family would, some day, reap the fruits of my precaution was already at that time only the superficial reason for my feeling more at ease, not the secret one. What was going through my mind can only be expressed in images and will earn me everybody's sneer: swathed in my insurance policies like the wealthy Egyptians in their bandages, I saw myself arriving safe and sound and dreamless at the other shore, yes, above all: dreamless. In this delicate armor I hoped to be invulnerable, even against the touch of eternity which I was never able to imagine as being other than resentful.

But this earth too had begun to weigh less on me. With Irene by my side, I ventured forth like a convalescent, each day a few steps further from the deliberately narrow circumferences of my existence, and last summer—I hinted at this already—I dared show my face, for the very first time in my life, under palm trees. Since Irene was an eager photographer, I could verify this impression with my own eyes. I did not like myself in her snapshots, if I may say so. I looked somewhat transparent among the exotic vegetation, as if one could neatly pluck me out with two fingers, and the background of palm trees would close once more, silently, like a curtain. But at that time the blue man had already appeared to me, had reawakened my fear, snatched it from my half-closed hand and away with him into The Unfathomable. It was like this: in the ground which I believed had become firm under my cautious step, a gap opened, gloating maliciously, and from it rose the sharply defined outline of that small, seemingly powerless figure. In reality he had been sitting there all the time— sat in fierce meekness, almost gruesome with reality, so close to our table that I could have photographed him; he would not have objected; indeed, as a barely tolerated street musician he had no right to object. If I had only done so! Then there would be no need to describe him—a feeble gesture when measured against the vast ambush into which he escaped—those empty southern streets, where he, crouching in a corner, brewed the potion to destroy my marriage, where he lurks to pounce one more time, trans- formed into a vulturelike angel to rob my fear of its last foothold, so that it may fall again into the abyss. I say this because anyone who has as little fear as he has to oppose life surely must have awesome connections, surely must be an ally of fear itself, and I know one day he will present this fear in a final reckoning the way one presents an exorbitant bill or a gun. I am convinced that with two moves he could change his singing saw into an instrument of murder. Had I only been able to pay him off! Or had I never thought of paying him off! Now he freely roams the world with my unconsummated offering, and, if I know anything about life, he will come back a November day like this one and demand a sacrifice I will be unable to make, because I do not know what else I could possibly give up. And then the little dike I have erected between myself and my fear will give way under this weight, under my eyes, and my eyes will turn blind, and dreams will begin—which I dread more than anything else.

The scene is simple, even though it was new for both of us. After all, it was our first vacation on the Mediterra- nean—in fact, our first vacation together (the honeymoon had to be postponed because of the annual balancing of accounts) and probably the last one for some time to come—I had my wife's condition in mind only. Irene and I—my wife's name is Irene—had just returned from the bullfighting arena. It had been frightful entertainment but Irene, against my protests, had insisted on going. And now, I must say, we were both glad to have escaped the bloodred sun (seats in the shadow were beyond our means). We had washed up a little—it was a dusty day—and we were sitting downstairs on the hotel patio drinking tea. The place had been graced equally by nature and by history. People said that in its better days our hotel had been the lodging of the Grandees whenever they attended the Viceroy's court, and something of their darkly luxurious spirit still hovered in the arches which circumscribed the courtyard like raised eyebrows. The weight of these arches was softened by airy greenery spreading in pots all over the tiled floor, and here and there, from frail foliage gigantic blossoms burst forth. In the center a fountain—forever catching and delaying its exhaustion in delicate jumping thrusts—played against a square piece of sky which in the cool evening air took on a blue color once more. All day long the sky had been white like molten steel and had mirrored itself dully in the arena. Perhaps two or three other couples occupied the tables, among them an English pair to whom we nodded a greeting. A three-man band, all guitars, I think, played for us rather listlessly, trying to make up for their lackluster performance with loud costumes. I must not forget to mention the palm tree which rose a few steps away from where we were sitting. It was a remarkable creature: its small fronds, thrusting into the sky, looked as if they'd been soldered on and chafed audibly against the evening breeze; the disproportionately tall trunk however, tapering below and painfully enlarged in the middle, made you think of smooth concrete and looked like a snake that, rearing for attack, had been petrified by sudden torpidity after devouring its prey. That was the scene and, content to have escaped a much worse one, we stirred in our tea cups.

I felt a sting right away, when I saw him pull his chair closer—that is, into the open space near the palm tree— murmuring a barely audible apology; instinctively I reached for my wallet. He was a street musician: as if this were to bring about a miracle, he bent ceremoniously over the black box he had pulled on his knees, a box that looked like a child's coffin; with both hands he seemed to smooth further the lacquer already worn down along the edges to a brownish sheen, and finally he opened three clasps; their silver color, too, had faded to let a yellow brass shine through. I watched the reluctant movements of these hands because I don't like to look into people's eyes prematurely, particularly not into those of strangers. Out of a glance back and forth may grow infinite commitments. But gradually I realized that to continue watching these hands could mean an involvement too; for these were hands possessed with authority, yes, they even seemed like independent beings, I'd almost say: human beings, but human beings of a more delicate species, though animal by definition. Not that they were delicately made: on the contrary, they showed traces of a lowly background—calluses, knots, brittle veins, a tendency to gout; but these marks were secondary to their way of moving, which indeed was most delicate: they bestowed upon the act of opening the clasps, the emerging of the instrument from its velvet shell, the clarity of great humility or great cruelty. The blue velvet, crushed to a lighter shade, was threadbare like the cuffs going along reluctantly with the movements of the hands. Once the box had been carefully placed on the tiles and the instrument lay across the man's knees, it was a saw, no more than a saw-blade in a wooden handle that had a smooth sheen on the inside. It startled me because I had assumed it to be a violin after my first glimpse caught the violin bow inside of the box. Its narrowness to be sure made you think of a somewhat stunted, even a soundless violin, which, considering the nature and movements of these hands, should not have surprised me at all; in a more alert state of mind however, I could have known that no such instrument ever existed. But I felt limp, the bullfight had taken its toll, and besides there was a sudden silence (the band had stopped playing) in which not even the sound of the spoon stirring in my wife's teacup could be ignored; how much less, then, any kind of music, however thin it might be. Given the slow motions of this musician, settling things quickly appeared unlikely, and I withdrew my hand from my wallet. But somewhere in my chest remained an uneasy feeling about the presence of this man who had to choose of all places our table for his perform-ance, when there were other guests with a sense of humor who were more effectively armed against such surprise attacks.

When the saw finally lay across his knees he no longer hesitated but began to play. With his left hand he held the instrument slightly at a distance, leading the bow across the smooth side of the sawblade, which was a very ordinary sawblade. Under the bow's touch a crystal clear and some-what hollow sound arose which belied the dullness of the tight fiber and followed by the pressure of the left hand quickly bending the metal, the sound was drawn out into that famous whine so characteristic of this art. I need not describe it; everybody will have heard it at some fair or small variety show. I was resigned to listen, praying only for the by-now irrevocable performance to end soon, so that my tip, the whole purpose of all this, would reach its destination. My attempt to communicate with my wife about the amount met with absentmindedness which, when I insisted, gave way to an expression of such unmitigated resentment that I could do little else but follow her stare and contemplate the figure of the strange musician.

I no longer had to fear that he would return my gaze. He was utterly engrossed in his playing—I would say enthralled to an amusing extent, considering the kind of sound he produced. He produced it with a painfully tense expression which brightened ever so lightly, almost suggesting a smile, when the whine had reached its peak. But he took it back immediately, darkening it with the next bend of his head, listening for a new figure of sounds, as if it were not the work of his own hands. His playing was composed of half–elations and half–despairs, small thrusts pulsating through it as the shadow of a muscle moves through a lower marine animal. His tune consisted of attempts to reach a small perfection which, once achieved, he abandoned reluctantly and then with a new grip of his left hand he tore himself away, so to speak, as if it had not been the familiar hum of the saw but the whispered insinuations of an evil spirit. He kept his thin, sharply defined eyebrows knit together, but the eyelids, the largest I have ever seen in real life and not in a painted face, remained as quiet as if they had been open.

You must not imagine his tunes were original or at least very recent ones. They were popular songs from the thirties or forties, no doubt familiar to him from his younger years, whereas I knew them only as tunes without words. The man could have been thirty–five as well as sixty; now and then something in the motions of his yellow face hinted at a much older age, or even an illness. The skin stretched over his skull, taut to the point of tearing, and at cheekbones and chin, where it threatened to wear through, it appeared very calm with a gleam like the cutting edge of a knife over it. So obstinate was this face, it seemed to know no fear. I shuddered at the meticulousness with which this man bowed his instrument, in itself an instrument for cutting, for murdering verdant life. It unnerved me, as would tenderness toward a criminal.

Only gradually did it dawn on me that the man was a blue man. To protect myself against Irene's bad mood I had looked into the blue sky, tapping my fingers on our metal table. I stopped only when I realized I was tapping the beat of the singing saw, and then I noticed: the man, too, was blue. His blue had nothing to do with the late afternoon blue reflected now in the basin of the fountain: his was opaque and worn; it faded into a gray—dove-colored I called it to myself, so that I could confront my wife later on with an appropriate word. It was nothing but the faded blue of his pinstriped suit which had an old-fashioned, large cut—with wide lapels that reminded me of a uniform and of the fact that the man most certainly had no other suit. It was barely holding together and probably got pressed into its vague creases every night, between mattress and spring of some poor bed. The rustcolored silk tie bulged a little above the yellow-ribbed shirt and the high buttoned boots rested on the ground, as if enjoying a special grace. I could not imagine how the blue man had managed to treat these boots with such care in a country like this one, but that's the way they looked: very old and very well cared for. The cuffs of his trousers were much too large and swayed high above the thin ankles. Pain, if this man suffered any, certainly must have made him less sensitive by degrees. The coins my left hand had singled out in my pocket need not make up for all his wants.

I almost said he joined us at our table. But that would not be altogether precise. When he had finished his piece, he rested his saw between his legs on the chair, put his bow across his knees and moved a little in our direction without coming closer. It was only a tiny gesture toward us but one not to be ignored. I confess that it startled me because now I forsaw that the sweaty tip in my hand would never do; preoccupied, I hardly noticed that he had begun to talk to himself, but to himself with us. He now had his eyes open without lifting them to me or even to my wife, but he nodded frequently. He nodded as a way of encouraging himself, because he obviously felt that he was intruding; he seemed to be used to that assumption and tried to make up for it a little with his music, although he must have known that he made it worse. I had no doubts that he was speaking Spanish, a language which I barely understand, especially not in the local dialect, and I looked up into the sky in order not to shame him with deceptive interest. Only when I noticed my wife who was blushing nod in her turn, was I obliged to listen more carefully and discovered that the little man was speaking French, or whatever he considered to be French. Apart from the faulty pronunciation, it was an overly correct French, even formal, which employed phrases familiar to me through business correspondence, meaning little more than paper rustling, a polite filling of empty spaces such as exist between strangers. Later I asked Irene what the blue man had actually said, since I had not been able to put his words together, not even after noticing that they were in French; but she only said—"Oh, go away," she said.

I rack my brains, but I only succeed—now that Irene and the child have left me (little did I know that her request to leave then had been meant seriously)—I only succeed in remembering things the blue man most definitely did not mention. He did not talk of his life or tell a story or mention his name—did not ask for anything. At the time he seemed to be congratulating me on my wife, whispering how immeasurably fortunate my circumstances, because—and this was obvious—though it was my wife who nodded in response, I was the one he really was talking to. But in the case I do not understand why she nodded because it is not proper to nod your approval to compliments directed at your person. On the other hand, Mediterranean people have a ready tongue when they see something beautiful, whether or not it is within their reach. But right away I had an inkling that the intrusion of this musician would cost me a pretty penny, although I was unable to estimate its entire price: the disenchantment of my marriage and of my security, the loss of my customary life. Indeed I narrowly escaped being fired at the office, because a man deserted by his good fortune will be deserted by everything else. So far I have managed to stave off this ultimate dread by steeping myself totally, almost blindly into my work; but just because of that I probably ruined all my chances for promotion. Whoever works as hard as I have these last weeks, my superiors will say, must have a guilty conscience, he deserves mistrust and will have to be watched closely; I alone know that it is close watching from which I have to fear everything.

When the blue man had ended his speech he gave an encore, for my wife, as far as I could understand. The silent complicity into which he had apparently managed to draw all of us present had the effect that, to my greatest bewilderment, the three-man band, at the wink of the proprietor, positioned itself at our table and started to accompany the next piece on the saw with all aspects of Latin generosity. The blue man obviously accustomed to being just tolerated in this place, played, pale with embarrassment and with concentration, a piece called "Cucurucucu," I think. Whenever one of the guitarists warbled these syllables in an unstable tenor voice that broke into falsetto, the blue man's face contorted painfully, as if suffering helplessly on behalf of a perfection ruined by the intervention of this thoughtless voice. All the more intensely would he then jab at it with his bow twitching across the sawblade whenever the three costumed men, more condescending than courteous yielded a solo to him. They even stepped back a little and their fat fingers strummed the strings more softly. I sat helpless, bathed in sweat, yearning for the end and yet dreading it: what use was my small change now; the singing saw had cut too deeply already.

At first he did not want to take the money which I, advancing a few steps toward him, tried to slip into his hand. I had to wait until, with cruelly deliberate ceremoniousness, he had bedded down his instrument in the velvet box. I can still see myself standing in this garden which, all of a sudden, seems empty though I feel many eyes looking at me. Stooping a little, I stand next to the palm tree, trying to rest my hand on it, waiting, yet unable to sustain this innocent but, under the circumstances, pretentious gesture, while reaching out my other hand to rustle a few bank notes at the man and his quiet preoccupation. Perhaps I even turned around and smiled at someone? Never again since childhood days have I felt so useless, so much surrounded by nothing, as in this eternity of disregard; in reality it did not last more than a few seconds, seconds that laid open my complete defenselessness.

Then he took the money, actually took it in a hurry—I should have been puzzled, because the amount was such as one does not accept without comment, but he did just that, probably in order to cut short my wife's embarrassment. He made a deep bow and I looked down on the thin strands of his black hair which did not manage to cover the yellow shiny scalp. He even remained a few minutes in this position, as if he were obliged to offset my wretchedness with some of his own. Then he murmured something, picked up his box, and with shoulders drawn up, his head lowered, he stumbled from among the tables into the shade of the hotel lounge which swallowed him immediately.

I had sat down again. We did not talk. I waited for my wife to say something. I did not even dare stir my tea, I felt so damaged, so reduced to an animal state. I told myself that my mouth had an unpleasant odor and that things in the outside world hadn't the slightest difficulty in proceeding without me. However, this provided also a strange kind of consolation. Why had I taken this vacation, why come to this country? I no longer dared think of my wife sitting next to me. I had to make up my mind if everything would be over right now or a little later.

Then I got up, nodded quickly in her direction and rushed to the hotel entrance. Before entering into the street which gleamed like a desert through the arches, I turned to the man at the desk asking him breathlessly — ten rapid paces and I was already breathless — for the name of the blue man, which way he had gone, where he lived. Gonzalez was his name, more the man could not say, but he pointed into the open road where he had seen him vanish, engulfed by the motionless glare. As I began to run toward an ultimate brink, the emptiness of the world fell into my breast — no longer capacious enough, chafing against the air as if against something solid, yet never getting enough of it. I ran up and down the street, the houses moved further and further apart, my strides became smaller, they were loud, and the houses remained. Some people came toward me, some I overtook, they were corporeal in a ridiculous way, but my feverish anticipation

devoured them on the spot, they disappeared with a giggle
sounding like a hiss, perhaps I had bumped into someone, I
did not care. In years I had not run like this, I really
couldn't anymore, and my heart told me at every step that
it would burst; I told it: go ahead and burst, and this way
we ran on. My heart ran faster than I, no wonder, because
actually I wasn't running anymore, but was dragged along,
my legs kept me from falling down, and in my hand I held
my wallet; there was nothing else to do: I had to give him
everything. At the exchange rate it was more than a
thousand francs, a fortune for the blue man, more money
than he had ever seen. I kept nothing, only the airplane
tickets, not even the money for the hotel; we would have
to think of something, and if not—this would be the end;
Irene had not wanted it any other way. A thousand francs
for the blue man—in my mind I saw the shape of his great
poverty, detached from his body and now the shape of my
own perdition; this shape I could eliminate with one gesture of my hand clutching the wallet because now, at this
very point in my life, I must not yet lose it. Blind with
anticipation and throbbing with exhaustion my eyes grazed
along bare walls, empty alleys, where dusk nestled already,
blue and yet not quite the right blue. Everywhere I asked
for Gonzalez; again and again I hastily pronounced those
three syllables, dried saliva on my lips; oh, yes, my mouth
had an unpleasant odor, now I smelled it myself. But
Gonzalez was everybody's name here, nobody could help
me unless I knew something more specific; and I did not
even know what "singing saw" meant in their language: I
was sent to a toolmaker, a car mechanic, to a nightclub, a
record shop, but "singing" and "saw" nobody could bring
together, and everywhere somebody was called Gonzalez,
wore a mustache or raised his eyebrows without being the
One I was looking for. Finally a polite elderly lady under-

stood some French, understood better and better, had just heard the saw sing, and directed me into the next street: there was a house, a hotel (its name eluded me instantly), I could not miss its façade, in this hotel the little man sat every afternoon entertaining the guests with his art, just now she had passed by there, just now she had heard him. I had almost calmed down, my heart beat normally, I thanked her, turned around and went on my way. I found the façade; it belonged to one of the hotels frequented by the native people familiar with the establishment and in no need of being lured by advertisements and big signs. That was the kind of hotel where Irene and I should have stayed, where the blue man played without incidents; I almost heard his saw singing, and with my head high I entered through the portal, as if returning from a walk. It was a patio like ours; even the few guests sitting at the tables, staring at my wallet, resembled those at our hotel; the cement palm tree was thriving here too, only it leaned to the other side. There was also the fountain. It had been switched off. The English family nodded at me, the French one scrutinized me. I had entered my own hotel through the back entrance.

I slowly approached the table where we had been sitting. The waiter was clearing away some glasses, but we had not been drinking from glasses. He noticed me standing there, and with a gesture of his napkin–draped arm he invited me to sit down. I shook my head. The palm tree was leaning to the correct side now. I tried to hear something.

Dishclatter from the kitchen. In the dining room tables were being set. A fleet of napkins assembled in the bluish light of the tables.

Had he come back? The man at the desk said no. I put away my wallet.

Tomorrow, every day, said the man at the desk. In our

room I found my wife. She apologized for not having waited. She was very excited. From the souvenir shop in the hotel she had brought up a choice of handbags, moderately priced and handsomely designed handbags, a specialty of this country, and I was to help her choose one. My wife had to be treated with consideration now. Late in the night she said: "You were having a nightmare, I had to wake you."

After breakfast she decided, after all, on the other handbag. I paid for it. Now the money was no longer intact. You could no longer give it away in its entirety. But it was not my fault. In the afternoon we went on an outing. It was not expensive, but of course, something more had to be spent. Then we took our tea. The blue man did not turn up. My wife was very pleased with her handbag. It was our last whole day. Next morning I paid the hotel bill. We had to leave before lunch. The flight went very smoothly. These days I live in a small furnished room. Sometimes I see my wife from afar. She pushes the baby carriage, and from her arm dangles the handbag she chose in the end. Most of the time she walks faster than I do. Every day I keep telling myself that nothing more can happen to me now. But I don't believe it. I don't even know what will become of the life insurance now.

# REPARATIONS

## OR

# MAKING GOOD

In German there aren't many words with a double "d,"
but recently Armin Bleuler, fifty-two, an unobtrusive
man, was tried by a local court for *Leichenfledderei*,
corpse-looting. He pleaded guilty. The trial would have
been even shorter, if the court had not hesitated on
whether to try for larceny or for embezzlement. Which
goes to prove that we are dealing with a by now unusual,
highly specialized kind of offense—gone are the days of
luxurious burial gifts; indeed, the era of graves is coming to
an end—at most that era is represented by an official,
perhaps an employee of the crematorium, whose duty it is
to examine the preparedness of the dead for their—let's
say it—last journey; and it stands to reason that such men
should be selected most carefully. Well, Armin Bleuler,
unobtrusive, bald except for a reddish mustache barely
sticking, as it were, to his smooth face (which in itself had
the effect of a small miracle)—Armin was one of those

officials and a man of trust. The question arises whether he
had been wise to commit a crime nobody else could have
committed and to become delinquent for the sum total of
219.50 francs—the amount involved in the offense.

Morally and mathematically there is no question.
However, we have to keep in mind that "corpse-looting,"
ugly as it may sound, is only a word. It sits badly with a
living body, as almost all words; it hides a problem that
cannot be resolved conclusively through language—not
even through the merciful verdict of the court: four
months on probation. A conscientious civil servant like
Armin does not do anything senseless; but it can happen
that any given system of actions, though meaningful in
itself, can grow to become a threat to the larger system
upon which it was nurtured; a healthy active organ may
then turn into a cancerous evil, and an honest man over-
night into a criminal, even into the victim of his own deed.
That is entirely a question of the systems involved. But we
do not want to operate here with a double standard of
morality, and we are also far from applying social criticism. Armin would not have consented to either. That he
stands dumbfounded before his own deed does not,
according to him, diminish its gravity. No man in town was
less inclined to take morality lightly and not only does he
not know about social criticism—he does not want to
know about it. He admits his guilt, includes with peculiar
emphasis also his spouse—that's right, she was sentenced
to three weeks for receiving stolen goods (also a suspended
sentence); his only ambition after that was to be a pauper.

So the court allowed him to appear as a victim, since,
strictly speaking, there were no others. Armin, to be sure,
had looted the bodies but had not really taken anything
away from them; after all, they were dead; just as he had
not stolen from the relatives who had already renounced in

writing the misappropriated goods. However, they had wished for them to be consumed by fire together with the dear departed; in that respect Armin had opposed their final wishes and offended piety. Justice had to take her course as best she understood, and Armin took it like a man. Moreover, he had someone to blame it on, as somberly and silently as men from around here blame somebody else for their fate.

Armin was the first of seven children, he still is, to be precise, since his parents and siblings except for two are still alive; they had to see this day. His father worked in a foundry, more than once out of work during the critical 1920s and early 1930s, more than once tempted to fling his ability to work at the feet of his contractors, to whom the economic crisis did not seem to matter so much: but it was the only thing he owned. He had to learn that as a person—the only thing that remained in those dark days was strong language and his wife's consequent reprimands—that as a person he was completely dependent on his ability to work. One could finish him off simply by not buying it. The necessity of selling oneself and the inability to do so is a profitable lesson for strong dispositions only, but oppressive to the pride of the weak.

Since for many years this pride had no other outlet than the marital bed it comes as no surprise that God would bless such a union. That, at least, was the conviction his wife held. She supported his self-esteem as best she could even if the blessings produced with that wounded pride became a burden. She saved him from despair by giving it another direction and, from one childbirth to the next, a higher meaning. God mercifully took unto Himself one or the other baby before it was old enough to sin against Him, and Armin, a resourceful child, from the time he was six years old was helpful in swaddling and disciplining the others.

For a long time father Bleuler was in danger of drowning in liquor, nevertheless rarely missed a sober occasion to reproach his children for being "children of drunkenness." But then circumstances permitted him to be once more an employable laborer, permitted it beyond expectations when the economy, driven by the generals' wishes and accompanied by the mothers' prayers, once more rewarded loyalty and fitness with hard cash. Father Bleuler worked once again as a founder, with all his might, got rid of his working energy and therefore of all inclinations toward alcohol, coitus, or rebellion. He saw to it that the lessons he had drawn from life were applied to his children, and readily helped along with his own hand; he chastised his own flesh and blood wherever he could find it, and straightened it out, body and soul. Soon the children learned, first the oldest, that there was but one way to avoid the worst in life and *that* was the way *up* — mother had always said this and meant something pious, but she did not exclude material implications. That such a hard school for life could possibly have warped Armin, the defense attorney cautiously tried to suggest to the court; cautiously, because one must not shake the concept of a school for life as such, held dear by the court. He therefore used proverbs or quoted the classics whose wisdom is unassailable. For example, too sharp an edge, turns jagged; or, a bow drawn too tight will snap. . . .

A lot could be said about Armin's subconscious drives without saying anything that wouldn't be better formulated in modern textbooks, even if it is hardly ever accessible there to the one who really needs it. In its most condensed form Armin's concept of life probably sounded like this: anything but manual labor! He began as a gardening apprentice; then he found employment with the city who hired him for the care of the public gardens, later for the so-called provincial exhibition, and after the outbreak of the war for service in the cemetery. Even as an employee he was on the lookout for any opening within the crematorium crew, and finally, in April 1943, it happened: the administrator of the main cemetery offered him a raise from employee to civil servant and Armin himself had the privilege of performing the last honors for his predecessor at the cremation furnace. Indeed, through the spyglass he watched with his own eyes the fire consume the one who had made room for him, his benefactor. Maybe the court could have reflected for a moment on the thoughts that might have crossed Armin's mind. Guilt feelings? Malicious pleasure? Reverence? A little of everything? Armin himself had had a severe father; here a father figure was burning down to ashes and he was even paid for looking on; the mere thought makes a soul sweat, but Armin kept his feelings in check with a mixture of respect and scorn—without which his crime could not possibly be understood.

Respect above all else.

Here we see Armin on a work day during his best times. Normally ten, sometimes a dozen bodies, all of them unfamiliar to Armin, required processing. But Armin does not treat them as such. Like a good host he meets each one outside the door to the crematorium almost imperceptibly raised to Byzantine status—and takes his hands out of his pockets for the occasion. Correct, there's one coming right now, Armin has a feeling for it. Far ahead the hearse is turning into the cypress-lined avenue. Look at that hearse! After all these years of service Armin is still unable to hold back a frown. It is neither fish nor fowl, this black delivery van, a construction devised by a bad conscience, that's what it is; its functional box shape a mockery of the piety which is embossed on the rear door in the shape of two crossed palm branches (in older models it is cut into the frosted pane). No more tassels, no black horses with heavy steps, no flowers carried in the open, and no bared heads. Out of respect for death Armin tries to render his expression as lifeless as possible. A hearse that moves through traffic like any ordinary car! Except for the eternal headlights—as if to say: another law rules here! And yet, it is only a purely decorative gesture, one no traffic light will yield to. Hence the indecent speed with which the car now passes through the cypress avenue, as if it were a test track and the driver in the cemetery of all places had to make up for time lost on the road. Also, as on every Friday, Armin notices from afar the layer of dust on the black finish; it gets washed only once a week, as a rule on Saturday. For Armin that is not enough; in a minute he will pass a reproachful finger over the fender which stops abruptly in front of him, and he will pay no attention to the comments of the driver and his assistant who get out and tear open the rear hatch as if they were delivering some kind of freight. That is the way the coffin is pulled out of the securing straps, dragged past Armin through the door and put down with a thud; in this moment Armin closes his eyes and hopes that he will die in the country.

Armin is still aware of the dignity of death and "to be aware of" is more than knowing, it is a form of suffering. As a consequence Armin suffers under the quantity which his duty as an official imposes on him; as a consequence he does more than his duty and sets up a somewhat symbolic limit to that imposition. He decorates the morgue with flowers and old-fashioned color prints. ("St. Francis preaches to the fish") and makes it a genuine living room

after the model of the American funeral parlors on which
he had looked up some literature. All this love and care is
greatly aided by the abundance of death paraphernalia,
since there is always a surplus of flowers from the more
affluent cremations that can be used for the poorer dead.
The chauffeur and his helper pay no attention to such
things whenever they throw rather than put the coffin
down, but the mourners appreciate it when they come to
discuss final arrangements and to cast a long, last glance at
the departed. Then Armin usually leaves the door to his
office ajar—he has his own office next to the "living
room." He knows that the mourner likes to be alone for
that moment, but not too much alone. The paper rustling
in the next room maintains, without disturbing, a connection to the world of the living. The papers again, for which
Armin is the official in charge, are necessary in order to
settle some formalities after the bereaved is done with his
tear-filled glance. For example: is it the will of the
mourners that the dear departed take with him/her also
the wedding ring and/or personal jewelry which Armin
has noticed on his/her person? If yes, would the bereaved
party kindly indicate that wish by a signature? If the
answer is no—there are valid and emotional reasons to
save a precious memento from the fire—would the
bereaved party also sign, but on the yellow form? Armin
would then re-enter the "living room" and deliver the
desired item. He takes along, without the righteous heir
noticing it, a piece of soap; wedding bands are not always
easy to remove. Never did it happen—this for the court's
record—that Armin would suppress the existence of a
valuable piece on a body. Whoever identified himself as an
heir was looked after. But when even the soap would not
help, as happens, Armin used no force. He would return to
his office and say literally—witnesses have confirmed this

noble phrase—that the dear departed would not give up the ring but be faithful beyond fire and grave. In case the mourners failed to understand this, Armin would bow his head regretfully. One thing is clear—and this aspect alone puzzled the court—even if the ring had been requested but was too firmly embedded in the flesh, never did Armin pocket what he had denied to the bereaved. He honored fidelity under all circumstances, saying never did a ring like this disappear conveniently into the waistcoat pocket. It was to remain his/her property.

That you could be unfaithful with a ring on your finger, Armin did not want to know. So great was his innocence.

Enough of the respect. And the scorn? For the professionally trained eye it may lurk in the bitterness with which Armin defended marital fidelity of corpses so completely unknown to him. First of all, it should be noted that he took the respect still further—for the taste of some laymen and the court, a step too far. Unfortunately no psychiatrist was granted the opportunity to voice his opinion on the fact that Armin, his eyes firmly on the fireproof spyglass, would watch the transfiguration of his dead more often than necessary, as often as business permitted, which in his exaggerated piety he would slow down now and then. By the way, it is not true that the coffin, under the impact of heat, always opens with an explosion, and that the deceased, surrounded by his flaming hair, rises one last time; that may happen once in a while, but that was not what Armin was waiting for. However, something essential must have touched him whenever he stared into this roaring and whistling inferno—the whistling is especially hard for the layman to imagine!—otherwise he would not have observed this duty so painstakingly and heaved a sigh when the unknown human image, faithful or not, had burned down to glowing ashes and the fire roared in a vacuum, so to speak. Something had to be finished, done away with, whistled into extinction, again and again, every work day, but since the psychiatrist did not make a statement, one can only guess what.

One can always guess and by doing so touch upon an area no less sensitive. Armin, raised by a heavy hand, hoped for some firm ground under his feet when he got engaged to a decent girl in the fall of 1942, after Hitler's assault on Russia. At this point, some remarks about the accomplice, Mrs. Sabine Bleuler, are in order. Armin had met the née Oggenfuss in a wealthy West Swiss household, where he, to bolster his wages as a grave digger, cared for the garden after his working hours. The garden could almost be called a park and contained rose bosquets, a rock garden, and even a small orangerie attached to an 18th-century pavilion. Since the supply of labor had all but dried up, the able-bodied, serious young gardener was well liked and treated with as much familiarity as the distance of class and lifestyle would permit, a distance which Armin sought to diminish by his hard work, a courtesy of the poor. That he kept company with Sabine, the maid, who during the war rose to the position of nanny, met with the greatest benevolence which Armin never took advantage of. He would not have known how! Swaddling little sisters, ordering them around, that, yes. But if one has been brought up not to harbor sinful thoughts, one begins to imagine, since one cannot prevent it, unnatural, outrageous things which are impossible to think of in connection with the self-assured behavior of grown womenfolk, the gentle swaying of their tightly laced behinds, because one must not; giving oneself orders won't do anymore, and, in the long run, not even self-abuse. As a consequence Armin was so inhibited that even a plain girl like

Sabine felt absolutely safe with him, safe and a little embarrassed, for, as we know, male innocence is an explosive and unreliable matter. Thus Armin struggled with the cross of first love, the most abominable form of solitude that can befall a person with a strict upbringing, for he would never dare attribute to the other the desires he harbors in himself, desires over which looms heavily the paternal judgment on smut and filth: the threat of that sin that gave life but must not know of life in its true sense (for economic reasons), and therefore does not wish to know (for moral reasons). Armin did nothing to be ashamed of with Sabine; on the other hand he did nothing he did not actually feel ashamed of. He had one restless night after the other. All the gardening did not help— three hours and more on long summer evenings. However, he got used to considering his innocence and the embarrassment it caused him and Sabine as a pledge to success, to the better life he dreamed about—represented so portentously in the style of the manor. Armin earned for his care of the roses, thorns included, two hundred francs a month; at that time it was a respectable sum for a laborer establishing with his employer not just a personal but almost a cultural relationship.

Nevertheless, Armin was surprised when one last day of the month in the spring of 1943 he was asked to come to the office of the master—an important man in the construction business, his name does not matter. On the way there Armin kept asking himself what rumors could have sprung up, who had slandered him or even found out the truth as far as his burdensome fantasies were concerned; for Armin could no longer exist without a bad conscience. Therefore with a trembling conscience, Armin faced the master builder, too nervous to notice that those diplomatic gestures, too, seemed a trifle more angular than usual.

From the corners of his eyes he observed the gentleman's room, the shelves full of annual reports and the classics; even the setting sun had a sheen nobler here than in the garden. There were good reasons for the silence in the house, because the master had sent wife and children into the mountains, to the lake of Thun, where he owned a chalet, where the air was purer and the cream not rationed; this way he saved himself a big move in case the Germans invaded, and he was on constant alert to join his loved ones in such an emergency. The chauffeur therefore kept the convertible ready to start and had even been exempted—the master had the right connections—from military service for that purpose, as had Armin, by the way, who as grave digger fulfilled a vital military function and, moreover, was in possession of a yellow armband which authorized him to evacuate two street blocks. The master himself was a colonel; he had known how to give his construction firm some military significance, and on some weekdays he paraded his uniform in the car. "Others though will die below," it had said in the anthology for ninth grade which Armin had been privileged to use in school, others have their seats prepared, near the sybils, near the queens; and then, as far as Armin could remember, there was talk of light hands. A beautiful poem, it contained the order of a whole world. The faraway chalet in Sigriswil was such a sybil's throne, although the colonel's wife was called Cordelia. It was not to be taken literally, but in a higher sense, and you could sympathize with it. Armin performed Herculean labors sympathizing—and the master's garden thrived on it.

The master thanked him for it. And yet, as it gradually dawned on a pleased and bashful Armin, this was not the main reason for which he had been asked to see the master. After fifteen minutes of real conversation, the master,

keeping his eyes on his fingernails, came to the point. An
accident, he said shrugging his shoulders, had occurred in
the manor, which could easily grow into an annoyance and
was undesirable for the cause of peace, for domestic peace
too. More precisely speaking, it was growing in the womb
of Sabine, and therefore he, the master, was asking his
gardener for advice, man to man. Stunned, Armin replied
that this was out of the question, since he had not touched
Sabine, except for smooching a little, as happens between
betrothed people now and then, but that, too, in modera-
tion. As for the rest—he had tried to wipe those thoughts
out of his mind. Whereupon the gentleman, with a thin
smile, replied, that he personally would be inclined to
believe this, but that other people might have little faith in
such restraint. Would Armin not contemplate a speedy
marriage to forestall the inevitable rumors—even though
among people of higher class, to be sure, those rumors
would not be considered a blemish on his reputation? That
it would not be to Armin's disadvantage. He, the master,
pledged himself to present the child-to-be with a chris-
tening gift of 10,000 francs. The parents, of course, whose
own well-being cannot be separated from that of the child,
could dispose of the money as they saw fit. But far be it
that he, the master, should pressure Armin into a step that
he could not take in good faith. That the request for time
to think it over which he read in Armin's eyes was already
granted; Armin did not have to ask for it. Would he now
talk it over quietly with Sabine. And furthermore, the
master would look forward to a continued work relationship with a couple so dear to him and think of ways to
render life more agreeable, war or no war. That he would
even be willing to have the pavilion near the rose garden
cleaned out and prepared as a live-in apartment and cozy
lovenest without Armin having to give up his position with

the city administration—grave-digging, after all, was a service to life, too.

The silence in the mansion by now had become so deep that Armin felt like screaming. What the master could read in his eyes was by no means a request, but naked under-standing struggling between shock and the urge to commit murder. But he wrestled down both, one after the other, gave his master no further look or greeting, but left with heavy steps to search the silent house for Sabine. Up and down the stairs the avenger dragged his dirty shoes, across deep pile rugs, as if they had been put there to wipe his feet, did not stop outside the master bedroom, spat on the damask, crouched into every nook and cranny and haunted the attic. Finally he found her in the basement. She had not been hiding, she was ironing, as always at this time. This dishonest orderliness enraged Armin more than any-thing else.

Without a word he dragged her away from the ironing board out into the open space which he needed to slap her face. Strangely enough, even the hardest blows fell into the deepest silence, except for their heavy breathing. By this kind of treatment Sabine of course did not cease to be pregnant—in a manner of speaking, quite on the contrary; by and by the rage of the gardener while hitting away took a very unexpected turn and led to intimacies; nothing prevented them from being continued on top of the laun-dry basket, until the thrashing could no longer be distin-guished from a fierce wedding, the breathing no longer distinguishable from an exultant sobbing. This turn, which exhausted Armin's wrath together with his body, did not take away one jot from his contempt: indeed, given his kind of upbringing, it even confirmed it. However, with a chill his reason returned—it too had taken on a different quality, a touch of the cruelly practical. Of course it would be dishonorable to accept the master's offer, but what good was honor now, what good was it to him? The collapse had opened his eyes: it smelled of self-deceit and pious stupor, this troublesome respectability, of the staircases of his childhood, of cabbage, turnips, and cheap floor wax. To the first principle of the pious climber: never be a laborer! now was added a second one which did away with piety and could be interpreted as follows: get whatever you can—go the whole hog! That day in May left only the climber in Armin. And whoever has had the privilege of maturing in a glass house rather than on the back stairs—may he cast the first stone.

With respect to worldly wisdom Armin had collected relevant data not only in the master's study but also on top of the laundry basket. Above all, that one can make a person with an even worse conscience than one's own feel guilty rather profitably, payable in hard cash or in emotional currency—a respectable indemnity from the master and lifelong submissiveness from Sabine. Add to this that Sabine, under insistent questioning on the laundry basket, tearfully assured her Armin that next to his, the gardener's performance, the master's could not even be considered. Armin could enjoy this triumph only moderately; to his sensitive nose it smelled too much of whorish prudence, however it would do well as a trump against the master. As cynically as he could, Armin stepped up to him and declared the deal all settled, but with Armin's conditions: 15,000 francs for the woman, and no further services whatsoever.

A bitter pill for the master, but he had to swallow it. His pavilion remained empty, the roses suffered, blight spread among the trees. Years later, whenever Armin took a walk with his wife past the neglected garden, he noticed it with satisfaction. His wife's eyes, however, clouded over guiltily as on the first day. That's right: the child was stillborn; Armin had his 15,000 francs without any counter obligation. It did not even come as a relief; he reproached his wife with lack of trust, even selfishness: that she just hadn't wanted to part with the child to whom he would have been a good father.

Their marriage remained childless. After Armin had entered the civil service career it settled into well-heeled but persistent gloom, a kind of never-lifting mountain fog, where there is never real thunder and lightning. Those not too close to the couple had no reason to notice anything: Armin made up for his silent depression with liveliness and achievement. He cared for his dead, and even in the fire would not let them out of his sight. Only sharp or sympathetic eyes might have noticed the fluttering and brittle quality of his competence. However, he had no one but his superiors, to whom he gave no reason for closer scrutiny; no one whose sympathy he would ask for. He lost his hair; that was no disgrace—it happens to many.

Not to forget one detail: that day, on the laundry basket, he had torn off her engagement ring. You did it, with my ring on your finger! he said with extreme envy and horror. To his even greater horror his rage enabled him to inflict a second visitation upon the faithless one. He did not understand why, but he did it, she suffered it in tears, and never again in their marriage would it be so beautiful. Contradictions of life. Whenever Armin thought about it—he did so rarely, but for many years, mostly before waking up, yes, perhaps he awoke from the very sting of contradiction—he still had to struggle with his excitement and did not know what to do about it. It no longer took him to his wife—moreover she slept in the next room—but into the shower without delay and an hour earlier to work. That's right: the ring could not be found again, as if it were cursed. And yet, Armin searched his master's basement, inch by inch. He suspected his wife, as if she had swallowed it, which was absurd but led to a marriage without rings. Even later on the Bleulers wore no rings, a practice unusual in their circles. But Armin never cheated on his wife, not even during military service, and needless to say, neither did she. There was only that one time. On the laundry basket the Bleulers lived their youth; on the same laundry basket they lost it.

Get what you can—go the whole hog. Quite obviously, the hog wasn't as fat as Armin had hoped. Armin's little tree of life prospered and grew, if not into heaven, nevertheless from one rank in the civil service to the next higher. But the roots were diseased; with every increase in pension rights the unacknowledged question arose: what for? He worked as hard as if he had to annihilate the present, stunted as it was. But he was unable to look forward to the future which one acquires in this way, and the evil past did not become less by it either, just lightly covered over. Soon Armin's salary permitted Frau Bleuler to give up her own work, or rather, he did not allow her to persue work any longer. She was supposed to enjoy her home, busy herself completely with the care of the empty nest, and she did, whatever the expense. They could afford this and more. But the question: what for? was written in invisible letters on the walls of the new five-room apartment, regardless of the guests they hosted with such strain that they would not return, regardless of the philodendron and the old etching. Life had improved, but it really wasn't a life for anybody.

Let us return to the dead. In a way, Armin envied them because they had put it all behind themselves and looked as if their peaceful expression had been acquired honestly, while he had but his honesty and no peace. As an official he did everything to treat them with respect, indeed to defend them against the business-like behavior of the workmen and the processing circumstances. Hence the flowers in the "chapel," hence the reminders of things everlasting with which he decorated the formerly bare walls: color reproductions by Reni or Ciseri, but also more contemporary stuff like Hunziker. Without realizing it, he made this last waiting room before the furnaces look like his own four walls. But when the dead grinned—and very often they grin a few days after the transition; it does not happen on purpose and has to do with the irregular decay of tissues—when they grinned at him, from among the flowers he put around them, then something turned bitter deep inside Armin, and it is understandable if he watched them turn into flames and burn down to ashes, not quite with pleasure, but with agitated satisfaction. And finally it is understandable why he took off their rings first, whenever they came off easily, a bad sign in itself. It meant: I know you! why should you fare better than I did! and it had nothing whatsoever to do with stealing. The defense attorney, a man with a socially inclined imagination, had reflected a long time on whether to present these points to the court. But then he told himself that they would seem far-fetched and strained to the judges, and so hardly to the advantage of his client. Moreover, the defense attorney, himself still in the process of climbing the social ladder, had no intention of making himself appear ridiculous and hurting his as yet unestablished image. After all, he was a lawyer and not a psychiatrist; if one had wished to consult one, one could have done so, and he himself would have been all for it, if Armin had not put up an immediate resistance. He wanted a clean verdict, he said.

Well, there was very little that was clean or even clear about Armin's behavior, even if in the end it was not his fault. It would have been a relatively clean case if he had either let those misappropriated wedding rings—he never took other valuables—disappear as years ago the engagement ring had in the master's basement (unintentionally), or else made them into cash and taken the risk himself. But he did not do that. He delegated the responsibility to his wife, who had become a very proper middle-class lady, thereby taking a much higher risk, so that one either has to consider it a frame-up or else doubt the defendant's common sense. Not a conscious frame-up, certainly not. But if there is anything about Armin that deserves being called thievish, it must have been the utterly unconscious and therefore all the more gratifying *Schadenfreude* with which he sent his wife into her easily predictable undoing. The née Oggenfuss—this is on record and led directly to the couple's arrest—behaved so awkwardly in every junk shop she entered that even the first buyer should have smelled a rat. It is downright shocking and casts a sad light on the entire profession, that only the ninth or tenth decided to become suspicious of the blushing and stuttering Sabine, who had by no means picked up experience along the way, to call the police while he kept the stammering woman on the hook, until the first sergeant on the scene caught her red-handed. The plan succeeded. Finally she had come to fall over that symbol of fidelity denied to her, the fidelity she had betrayed once, inexperienced, in a state of dependence, and she had come to fall in a way she would have deserved in Armin's eyes way back then.

But with those roughly seventeen wedding rings— 219.50 sfr—didn't she also drag her Armin into the disaster? Well, that had been her Armin's very purpose— not conscious, but therefore more clever; and here the second and most important part of his scheming becomes evident. Nobody in his right mind would expect Armin to take revenge without having to pay for it at the same time and to suffer punishment—his scheme was, indeed, not only to become guilty, but to become the absolute pauper, and this included of course the loss of pension rights. The whole problem of making good is never quite that simple and unequivocal with repressed people like Armin, even if they labor a lifetime toward that goal; this life is not the noblest good, said the poet. The fact that his robbing the bodies struck a much harder blow to Sabine, completely dependent by now—in a less dependent state she would hardly have lent herself as a fence—was a not altogether unpleasant by-product of the whole unconscious setup. Once again Sabine bore the guilt, more than she could ever make up for. Of course he would not consent to being cheated out of this advantage by taking an analytical look at this scheme or even his marriage—hence his resistance to the psychiatrist. He insisted on the almost incomprehensible single occurrence of his prank, on its being just a tragic lapse, and from his point of view he was right. There was indeed a single event at the bottom of his thoroughly decent and joyless life, only it had already taken place in the master's basement and not in the house of the dead. As the innocent culprit, as someone become guilty in a mysterious way, in short: as a pauper he presented himself to his judges and wanted to be sentenced. The delinquent sum as such confirmed his indubitable decency: 219.50 sfr, as did the passion with which he defended his sobbing spouse at the bar. The fact behind this gala performance lurked something like a dubious vindication, a reparation from long ago, from as far back as his mother, if you look closely—making it all the easier for the vindicator to let the vindicated one stew in her sense of unworthiness—this fact the vindicator did not necessarily have to know himself. Neither did the court know it; it was too busy with its own emotion. It convicted Armin because it had to, in God's name, and demonstrated benevolence with a suspended sentence. Armin was to have his second chance.

And he did. The position in the crematorium was taken—well, at least that, in the name of piety—but the presiding judge himself had taken note of the man who stood there at the bar, steadfast, taking his sentence with a manly smile. His attitude in the courtroom had recommended him as a man of character. It was precisely the one-time offense which seemed to be a safeguard against recurrence, more so than a clean record, it was even better than a good deed which would tell less about its doer than is revealed in the course of a painstaking court action: in the case of Armin, nothing but the best, except for that ill-advised prank. The presiding judge managed to be informed by competent sources how and under what circumstances Armin was living. The philodendron was mentioned in that report as well as the spick-and-span kitchen.

If one takes into account the serious, indeed alarming shortage in our city police personnel brought about by the adversities of the times, Armin's further career can hardly remain in doubt. But the police superintendent, tipped off by his close friend at the court, did not rush into decisions. He had Armin put under discreet surveillance, ordered, so to speak, a trial period for the unsuspecting Armin. Armin carried himself above reproach. At any time he was ready to plough the streets (it was a snowy February) and got up every day at three or four o'clock in the morning, without complaint, to sand and salt the roads. No expression in his face led one to believe that he was really too good for this kind of work. He simply excelled as always: swaddling siblings, digging graves, pruning roses, even on the red checkered laundry basket, but let us finally drop that subject. After three months there could be no possible objection to his joining the police force. One of his first official duties took him to the crematorium—it would be overestimating bureaucracy to see any particular planning in that. He had to supervise the elimination of certain objects, those seventeen rings which the court had decided to turn over to the purifying flames—for the rightful heirs did not turn up and could not be found. To simplify matters they were to be put into a coffin; it so happened that it was the plain coffin of a Sister belonging to a Protestant order. She was eighty-three years old. Under the watchful eyes of the policeman, Armin's successor put the sealed package under the folded hands of the departed, who grinned at that. Armin in his new uniform did not even wink. He did not bother with the actual control of the cremation. Those times were gone for good.

Armin climbed to each of the next ranks in the shortest possible time. His father who had had to see his shame could now live to see this and enjoyed a tranquil happiness. Soon Armin's pension rights were as high as the earlier ones. His wife was no longer able to enjoy it. Within a year, only forty-seven years of age, she passed away. The operation came too late; Armin was on patrol duty that night. They say it was cancer of the uterus, quite common among women. Nothing you can do about that.

# BRAM'S VIEW

His picture still hangs on my wall, a round, brownish photograph from the first years of our century. The head looks out of the frame, upright and straight, but the eyes don't focus on the onlooker, they stare past him, a little to the right, with an expression as though it took courage to go through with this; however, this could be attributed to the strain of prolonged concentration on nothing but the photographer's hand which sticks out from under the black cloth, motioning: eyes this way. Keep looking this way, please. A photograph created the illusion, even back then, that the person in the portrait had a clearly defined goal, worth training one's eyes on, the limpid eyes of the Rüesch family. Even the children were made to pose as little sailors, for the grownups to remember, later for their own memories. Adults were expected to muster at least an expression that matched the outfit, even if they were from the rural interior—as thoroughly landlocked as the

Rüesches, typical Oberland farmers; at least that's what my mother said.

I'd never have the thought that he'd be the first to go, she said of the man in the picture. He was her uncle Abraham, called Brämi, whom she got to know when she was still a child, during vacations on the farm. I always thought the man was immortal, she said, the way he walked and carried himself. She said that the thought of death struck her for the first time in those days, and looking at Uncle Brämi she knew only one thing, it would never hit him. Brämi standing next to my father, the farmer next to the clerk, was like a picture of day and night. And I feared for my father in those days, I didn't really know why. I believe it was the trembling of his hand whenever he stroked my hair. He didn't really stroke it, she said, he was wiping something away. And his hand made you think of the paper on which he wrote, in his narrow office. I believe I wished him away, she said, that's why I was so afraid for him. I thought I would have to die because I couldn't stand that hand on my hair. I would have liked to have Uncle Brämi for a father; every time my father returned from trade school, Uncle Brämi would throw him against the barn door.

But that was not why I was fond of him, my mother said, and anyhow, it was before I was born. At the time my father was still a student. He himself told proudly how Brämi used to fling him against the wall, and for this pride too, I felt contempt for him. My father always had the consolation of coming away as the more refined of the two, when he wasn't up to Brämi's pranks. Once Brämi had set things straight, he could be talked to again. He had his own sense of humor, a kind of humor I've never found since. He'd turn a word around once, drop it or toss it down, and go on his way as if nothing had happened. You see, my mother said, it was as if somebody flicked a straw off your dress, in passing, without saying a word, and yet, to me, it would seem like a caress, much more than my father's whole hand was able to do when he left it lying there, still trembling from his writing chores. But Brämi's touch was a proof of life. I believe that's why I considered him immortal. He had lighter eyes than any of us, I'm glad you have them too, to some extent. And then he was the first to go, and like *that*.

It wasn't until I was sixteen that my mother told me about Brämi. One had to be old enough to understand, she said. But I waited in vain for her explanation. There didn't seem to be any, which my mother could have reconciled with her memory, the sparse recollection of a towering jovial farmer who had never picked her up in his arms, but whose presence my mother had felt, during those two vacation weeks, in a way she'd never again felt anybody else's presence. I was too young to understand, she said; all of a sudden he wasn't there anymore. Nobody wanted to tell me how and why: there just was this hole torn into my world.

I don't know if it was the women, she said softly, as if she herself were not a woman.

Today, she said, I can't imagine why this man should have had anything to fear from women. But the way he touched me, she said, and hesitated: I don't even know if he did, perhaps all my life I have only imagined it. If he had touched me, it would have been like a farewell, and that, perhaps is why it so affected me later on.

Never before had I heard my mother talk this way; I had hardly known of the existence of this great-uncle, the last Rüesch who was still a farmer like his forefathers. There was no opportunity to come back to the subject later, because my mother didn't have much longer to live.

For quite some time she had gotten into the habit of interrupting herself when she talked, in order to breathe. I took it for pensiveness, a mannerism even; but it was the beginning of the illness, of the shortness of breath that suddenly led to the end.

I've been living alone for a long time now, with a number of memories, to which my mother's memories have been added. To someone else they might seem like mere conjectures, but for me they have a powerful reality. Since my responsibility for my wife and children has been taken from me, I have free time and feel the need to concern myself with people who are no longer present, be it that their lives are continuing without me, be it that they have ceased to live; it leaves me, in mother's case, with the almost physical sensation that something about them has remained open, and is in need of careful restoration. Sometimes I dare to think that it's a worthwhile task, and that it will fill a void; as though every human being, at birth, were entrusted with a thought which he must leave behind when he dies, but which wants to be thought out to the end or at least elaborated on, to make the failure seem less harsh. Since I can't find such a thought in myself, or have perhaps lost it in the course of the past years, and since my profession claims only my surface time, I like to stay in places where a definite and violent sense of loss lingers, regardless of my own; and by and by I have made my mother's memories my own.

Among her possessions I found Brämi's picture—it has her handwriting on the back—the brownish, faded picture of the thirty-year-old man, who still had another decade to live. My mother seemed to be absolutely certain on one point: she refused to consider Brämi's end a disgrace. This refusal—I was not able to fathom its boldness during her lifetime—I've tried to buttress with investigations of my own. Because today I'm less indifferent to my mother's needs than in the years when I was too young to take them seriously; in those days, I, too, thought my mother was immortal.

Whenever I look at my features—it happens when I brush my teeth or wash my hands—I find that I've become my mother's son more and more with every year. I have to bear her features, and be responsible for them. I'm more than half a Rüesch, and I believe that inwardly, too, I've moved closer to that side of the family, in full awareness of the horror it implies. Without this horror—strange as it may sound—I could not have found the strength to go on living; for much has fallen away that I considered closest to me, and that is able to exist without me in an evidently much less troubled way. Therefore, in order to hand down anything of myself, I'll have to *accept* what was passed on to me. My mother couldn't give me her maiden name, although from the very beginning of her marriage, and certainly during her long widowhood, she was happy to sign it right after her husband's, my father's, name. My name is Bruppacher, nothing more. But since I learned to understand that the image of everything she'd ever lost was condensed in the image of her Uncle Abraham, and since I found it possible to share the feeling of total loss, I have decided to open the picture above my desk, as it were, and to restore a body to the head that stands there alone, in its thin frame.

I visited the village where my maternal forefathers were at home and farmed their land. I measured this land with my steps and learned to see it without the housing project that stands there now. I gained access to the house, the last house in which Abraham had lived; it presented no problem at all, given my distant kinship, although the present farmers were somewhat taken aback—the horror still echoes through the village, even if by now it has paled to a vague rumor, a piece of local history. They let me stand at the window which once belonged to the parental bedroom, and with an effort of the imagination I wiped away all the buildings and obstacles which the past fifty years put between my view and Brämi's. I saw what he had seen. I noticed that I had grown mature enough for this view, that all this time had had to pass, even my own irreplaceable life, until someone, I myself, was standing at this window once again to relive those lost minutes. By recording them I don't intend to revive bygone horrors. On the contrary, I wish I could dissolve the gloom of that bright day in July, in the same way Brämi knew how to take away my mother's fear of death, by touching her, when she was a child. I know my words are not endowed with the power of immortality. But they may reveal my compassion, which might have helped my mother to exist a little longer—longer, or at least at peace with herself. I must ask the reader to contribute his own kindness.

You stare from my picture, a thirty-year-old man: twelve years later you stared out your window—that was more than fifty years ago—in the early afternoon, a quarter past one. The time of your death was mentioned in the newspaper: a quarter of two, July 4. Did you know it then, as you stood next to your desk, looking out of the window, half hidden by the curtain, invisible to anyone who might have glanced back at the house? All you did was gaze. Your eyes were open, although your wife had wanted you to close them for a while; she seemed to read in your face that you needed a rest, that's why she and your daughters had gone ahead. You lay quietly until you heard the barn door. There were three of them, but you heard only the creaking of the door hinges; they should have been oiled a long time ago. You heard that they weren't talking, perhaps they didn't want to disturb you in case you had already fallen asleep. Only when you couldn't make out another sound, no matter how you strained your ears, not even a *stifled* sound, no footsteps—perhaps there was the distant barking of a dog, suddenly the faint humming of a flying machine in the sky, or maybe your ears were playing tricks on you—you couldn't stand the weight of the blanket any longer and went to the window.

Did it enter your mind to call after them? They were still close enough. Under your eyes almost, your wife, your two daughters walked toward the land, the tools on their shoulders. You knew exactly where they were going, you had talked it over. The stretch of meadow behind the edge of the forest, too, was simply called "the land." You knew what had to be done, it wasn't too much today. The day before yesterday, early in the morning, you had mowed the spot when it was still wet. Since then, the hot summer had set in. The day was bright but hazy, the weather would hold. All that remained to be done now was to turn the hay and to leave it, easy work, work for women. You also knew when they'd be back. They expected you to follow later, in an hour, maybe after you had rested, to lend a hand with the pitchfork, to show them that you were also quite adept at the light work.

But when you were standing at the window, in the silence of the house, not rested, not really in need of rest, you suddenly saw only one thing: they were going.

There were going off, treading lightly, the older woman, still young, and the two young girls. They were going away from the house, where they had told you to take a rest. After the meal, when your eyes had taken on a vacant look, they had agreed all of a sudden that you

needed rest. They had said it casually. A little startled, but
making a joke of it, you had agreed to lie down for a while.
You usually didn't do things like that. But why not, on this
hot day, when you wouldn't miss anything. Why not, until
the women had finished cleaning up, and had washed and
dried the dishes. Perhaps one of them was reading the
newspaper you had just put down. The mailman had
brought it before noon, and you had teased your wife
about him, as you did every day. To lie down now for a
little while was a novel thought, not at all unpleasant. It
had nothing to do with getting older, but rather with the
possibility of creating a new habit, one of these hot days.

Perhaps you'd said to your wife: it would do you good,
too. Maybe she'd laughed. Maybe the thought: I could go,
and she could come, too, it was like a flash in the guts. One
never thought of such things, in broad daylight, but why
shouldn't one think the unexpected, suddenly, and your
daughters were old enough, they wouldn't mind. Wasn't
there something festive in the air all of a sudden, something long-forgotten, a suspenseful yet comfortable rest-
lessness; as if the children weren't there at all; as if it were
one of the bygone days, re-awakended by the buzzing of
the flies? Perhaps there had never been this fresh new day,
only the fear of it, the jokes about it; did it have to take
years of daily routine to make such a day imaginable at this
very moment, and to lose the fear? You saw what the flies
were doing, it didn't bother you; you didn't swat them—as
you'd always done—at the high point of their buzzing; the
sullen expression on your face was suddenly *misleading*;
anyone who knew you well would have seen it. You took
the match out of your mouth, stopped smacking your lips.
Didn't you, once before, have the feeling in the middle of
your chewing, that the movement of your jaws was an
imposition; not the chewing as such, but its mindlessness?

All of a sudden you felt self-conscious. You got up, pushed back your chair, no more gently than usual, and said: "If you insist, I'll go and catch a little shut-eye."

And as he was standing there, about to turn away, he heard his wife say to their daughters: "We'll go ahead then."

He held on to himself so as not to freeze in his tracks, to move on, to head for the bedroom. He went up the stairs into a glaring emptiness. His feet carried him automatically, but the sound of his own breathing struck him as something annoying, something superfluous. Nothing had happened, but as he was climbing the stairs, he knew that it was all over and realized that there had never been anything. It was a total, yet utterly soundless, continuous collapse; he didn't even feel himself falling. But what began to spread around him was nothing but the mocking echo, the lackluster appearance of things. He felt as if he'd awakened from a forty-year long exhaustion, but for what; there was nothing left.

"We'll go ahead then." They were going ahead, then, in case he did finally lie down. The fact that he was going to lie down was reason enough for them to go ahead and start working. They had really thought he was tired. They had by no means seriously thought he was tired. It was simply more convenient for them to go ahead without him, to his land. When he thought, "they," he didn't think of them singly. He thought of them as he had never thought of them before: the thinking of a doomed man. It suited them that he stayed behind, he who was born here, who'd been the strongest in his class, had become a father, three times; the only son had not seen life, he'd taken him away from his wife, had buried him under the elderbush, she would never know where. He'd been a farmer here for twenty years, and had never noticed anything, had never wanted to know or notice anything, in his humorous way. Now he knew, there had never been anything, and they were going ahead.

He lay down on the bed that had been shared, grown habitual, and pulled the woollen blanket up to his chin. July, and suddenly cold. He watched himself going through these motions. He no longer knew the person performing them, and it wasn't worth the effort to know him. They were going ahead.

He thought of revenge for a moment only. It was a moment of intensely painful longing, to be able to think of revenge; he let it pass and lay still again.

The mailman came to his mind; from now on it could be the mailman, it could be anybody.

Then he thought about swimming; he had never learned how to swim—

In the picture of the thirty-year-old man, the three lines in the face of the Rüesch family are clearly discernible:

The first runs from the bridge of the nose into the cheek. In people whose name isn't Rüesch, this line curves to catch the so-called tear sac. In a Rüesch it extends straight down into the cheek. That would be the natural course of the flow of tears. But in the Rüesches there's only its dry bed. We're unable to weep. The line ends in the cheek; with the years our cheeks become hollow and make the eyes appear wider and lighter. The phenomenon has been called "God's eye." It can be found in two or three other families who immigrated from the Southern Alps four hundred years ago and were allowed to settle in the Oberland, not exactly in the most favorable spots. The Lord for whose sake they had left their Roman masters, would probably see to it that they prospered even in the shade; that's what the natives thought. They knew how to thwart the prophecy that the foreign brothers in faith were destined to become a great people. And the newcomers adapted themselves. They allowed their names to be molded into pronounceable forms—Rüesch is said to be Rusca—and they recommended themselves by their dili- gence and quiet ways. The Rüesches were assigned a few acres of marshy land and a stretch of wilderness which, with God's help, they turned into a garden, but the name *Gfenn*—swamp—has stayed with the land to this day. In the twenties a linguist described Brämi's dialect as "remarkably uncorrupted" and his features as "purest Oberland." Sectarianism subsided with the generations. Brämi's grandfather supposedly still showed the door to the parson, in all politeness, because he enjoyed his own and unimpeded access to Revelation. But Brämi's father had become a churchgoer, the only one in his family, for no trait of the kind is reported about his son Brämi. On the contrary, I know from my mother that he was said to have been a "scoffer." This gave his neighbors an explana- tion—they found a good many others afterward—why he had to come to such an end. My father, a Bruppacher, was a pious man, but that's not part of the Rüesch history, and moreover, my mother never took his word for it.

At one point Brämi was thinking of elderbushes; then only of the word "elderbush." He lay in his silence. The air or whatever faint draught moves the summer air, seemed as if shut off, there was no humming in his ears. Yet, together with the word "elderbush," and with a clar- ity for which there seemed to be no further space, he heard steps in the house, and other words he could no longer decipher. It was coming from the kitchen, but not for long. People seemed to be in a hurry to get away, there was an activity behind walls and floors which hastened toward

silence and total stillness, like the activity over a grave
that's being filled in. As if from deep down, Brämi heard
his house empty itself of human beings.


The second line in the face of Brämi as a young man leads,
as it does in all the Rüesches, from the nostrils to both
corners of the mouth, a little less pronounced on the left.
This makes for a distorted expression which could be mistaken for a manly smile, for a refusal to be easily
impressed. The Brämi of the photograph shows it clearly,
the seat of his sense of humor, or whatever my mother
preferred to take for a sense of humor. It's strange that the
corners of the mouth never make contact with these smile
creases, which, in fact, give way, increasing the distance in
moments of great merriment way into the hollow cheeks.
That is why the Rüesches' smile or laughter never takes
hold of the face, it is as if incarcerated; the entire area
around the mouth is one sharply delineated pit. I can
imagine the good times when this mouth used to play with
words, shuffle them back and forth, and twist them. And
yet, there is a remembrance that this face could radiate
warmth a warmth that touched—if no one else—the child
that my mother once was.

Brämi, like my mother, had a large, sharply cut nose,
almost winged, an aquiline nose, which he hides in the
photograph by having himself portrayed face on. With a
nose like that, my mother once said, it hadn't been easy for
her to find a husband, and I remember how those words
hurt me, not because of me—my nose doesn't hamper
me—but because of her marriage. My father, dead for
many years, was depreciated even more by this remark.
But I had never been able to feel with him. I only thought

of the choice my mother did not have in her life, and whose product I am.

This is where I started my tale once before. Here it was where Brämi, aged forty-three, heard the barn door and remembered that he hadn't oiled it. If it hadn't been for the suspense, the paralyzing suspense of a man whose eyes had just been opened to his own death, he would have felt a maddening anguish about this neglect; the kind of anguish that overwhelms us only when we're concerned with details, never with large issues; with the unbearable knowledge that they no longer matter, and with the for-ever invalidated notion that they might some day matter again.

To the eyes of an outsider who might have entered the bedroom right then, Brämi would still have had the impressive appearance of an Oberland farmer. It is terri-fying, yet relievingly comical, to think that I've even tried to imagine: what if it had happened, now? What if, at this moment, a stranger from the street had done the incon-ceivable and entered this house, climbed the stairs with the audible steps of living—what if he'd even been a burglar, almost as out of breath as Brämi in his bed. Would the stranger have been able to call him back? Could a word have been uttered, perhaps a scream that would have startled the towering man, would have shocked him back into his former life? The impulse to defend instinctively, at this last moment, what had been, and still was, his own, if only he gave himself a push? It's a hope against time and probability, I'd almost call it a temptation. Perhaps a cry for help—in one of my dreams I've even begged Brämi himself to cry for help, for no other reason. *Something* might still have happened. But Brämi kept silent. Obvi-ously he knew that it was too late for help, that he didn't

want it any more, no: that he was no longer capable of
wanting it. For this help would have had to come from a
motive too profound and beyond all reach: because Brämi
existed, because he was there: because he was wanted for
*that reason* alone, not out of, perhaps, pity, out of consideration, respect or fear; not even out of fear that he might
have gone insane. Not for a moment did he toy with this
thought, that much I know. It had been decided, it was
over. Nothing could have moved him again to call attention to himself. All that mattered to him was: his folks had
"gone ahead," once and for all.


The third line in the Rüesch face runs left and right from
the corners of the mouth down to the chin and around it,
making it jut out like a small immobile ball. There were
Rüesches, Brämi's father for example, who let their ball-
shaped chins be overgrown by a full beard. I first caught
sight of my own chin and nose in a clothing store. I was
standing, fifteen years old, in a new, light-colored suit,
between the mirrors as if in a magic hall. I watched my
face without looking directly at myself, terrified at the
thought that something would have to become of that face.
Against my mother's wish I insisted on the light-colored
suit, although it was intended for my confirmation. I
thought that I'd need a light suit for the festive occasions
in the coming years of my youth. And then, at the confirmation, I was the only boy in a light suit, and I felt
embarrassed; and it also looked as if my family weren't able
to conform to the prevailing custom. And those festive
occasions never really came about. Most likely it had to do
with my disposition and with my exaggerated hopes for
such events, but also with the conservative cut of the

confirmation suit, hopelessly out of style at the festivities
of the others. But perhaps I was just as glad to have this
reason for avoiding pleasure with its bluntness and ambiguities. Today it doesn't hurt so much anymore. And yet,
it's the only grudge I hold against my mother, that she
didn't insist at the time on my getting a suit with a
youthful cut at least, even if it pinched a little, whether it
was light or dark.

It takes three steps to the window in these farmhouse
rooms. Had Brämi shot himself, he would have fallen back
on the bed from which he was now getting up, putting
aside the blanket. He took those three steps calmly. He was
no longer thinking, he was only driven to *see*, to see his
family going away. There they were, walking along the
path leading to the willows, then around a slight bend
which would hide them for a while, toward the woods. In
those days, the path to the "land" led through a narrow
copse along the watercourse; it had been allowed to remain
there at the time when the land was being cleared. Behind
those trees was the spot where they took their midday
break on hot days. It was barely fifteen hundred feet to the
willows, the first gnarled vanguard of the woods. On their
strip of paler green that indicated swampy ground, the
willow stumps seemed to advance toward the three persons,
to wait for them in order to guide them around the knoll
and out of Brämi's sight, until that one last moment when
he would be able to see them once more, hopelessly
reduced in size, at the edge of the woods. On their shoulders they carried pitchforks and rakes which swayed a little
whenever they turned to each other as they walked. They
were actually joking, bantering, they could talk freely now

that he wasn't with them any more. His eyes walked along with their feet which were doing odd work; it seemed to him like a mocking, playful scraping in which the feet showed him their soles in quick succession. His eyes ran around their figures like a dog, trailing them right and left; they knew every inch of that remote soil. Here near the willows, plants were thriving which couldn't be found anywhere else, and which he'd always left standing when he mowed: globe flowers, cotton grass, orchis, white nettle, and, in one spot only, the insect-eating sundew. He'd shown these places to his daughters, but they hadn't been interested. He was fondest of the small patch of pointed, tough sedge and reeds at the edge of the row of willows, out in the open, in the sunlight. It was a small depression which absorbed the water from the woods, the water that ran alongside the willows and that had drawn a furrow in the lush meadow. The path that the women took led along this notch, which made you think of the marshland of the past.

Brämi could see the land as in a picture, an impression eased by the window cross. Woods and meadow filled its largest part, the rising ground didn't leave much room for the sky, yet enough to let an unimaginable, blindingly gray emptiness rise from behind the woods' horizon, and chisel its upper outline into jagged edges. Even the midday haze seemed not to soften them but to swathe them in a hint of smoke, leaving undecided from one flutter of the eyelid to the next, whether the phenomenon out there was one of complete radiance or of total darkness.

Perhaps it was the thought that this day already stood in flames which guided Brämi's hand. His hand reached for the pink cartridge on his desk, the cartridge he had once brought home in his overalls and forgotten after changing his clothes. And since one needs both hands for lighting a match, he stuck the cartridge in his mouth. His tongue felt the firm round tip, the cardboard tasted flat, acrid sulphur fumes from the short fuse stung his nose.

In school I had a teacher who encouraged precise observation. To this end he made us describe the igniting of a match. This alone was to be the theme of the entire composition. To help us toward accuracy, he gave us a few pertinent expressions. "Guideway" was one of them; it described the part of the matchbox which is equipped with the so-called "striking surface," and I received praise for comparing the part that actually contains the matches to a little drawer, and later for observing that a match that's old or has been wet will crumble in the act of striking, or will ignite with difficulty; I wrote something about "hissing." The word would have been more appropriate for a fuse, but our teacher insisted that we treat the striking of a match seriously and without straying from the subject, and that we shouldn't think at all of firecrackers, the kind we used to explode on the last schoolday before Christmas, that early morning when we also tried smoking for the first time. Our teacher demanded a single, carefully observed action which, greatly blown up in our composition, was to fill three notebook pages. And in contradiction to this topic, and to the fire warning he added to it, the very same teacher made us learn a little song from the exercise part of our song book, a round which went as follows: "It's matches, it's matches, it's matches we take; a fire, a fire, a fire to make."

Brämi's wife was called Lisette; his daughters were Anna and Gretli. His lips formed their names, the names of those

who were going farther and farther away, with that happy,
almost liberated step, while his teeth held on to the cartridge. When the flame had taken hold of the match, it
straightened and became still. Without looking he lifted
the little torch, careful not to let it die; this was something
he could still take care of. Their walking was barely
noticeable now, as if the path were being pulled out from
under their feet; a few more moments and the edge of the
meadow covered their figures. Brämi felt the breath of
heat against his thumb and forefinger. Then his fingers did
what he did not need to order them to do. They passed the
remaining flame on to the brittle black fuse under his eyes.
He had to aim a little, focus his eyes sharply; at such close
range he saw only in a blur that the end of the string
caught the spark and began to sputter. With a final impa-
tient gesture he flung away the match. Closing his eyes, he
smelled his singed skin, it had smelled like this at the
blacksmith's. "Hoof shavings," he thought, and heard, at a
great distance from the crackling of the fuse, the buzz of
another flying machine. From the biting pain in his fingers, which he held open in the air, something like hilarity
came to him, pulling apart his pinched lips. And behind his
eyelids rose the image of a great gentleman who like
himself now, was resting his fists on the window sill. He
was allowed one more wish. He wished that they would
turn now, at this very moment, and look back at this
house; not for his sake, but to see how quietly it was
standing there. He was prepared not to watch the fulfillment of his wish, to keep his eyes closed. But he granted
himself the wish, giving in to it with all his soul, the soul
which he suddenly felt again, as a heavily leaning,
exhausted body; with this wish his soul had come back to
him once more, and with it an intense longing. He leaned
his forehead, his face toward the distance that separated

him from his family, who had surely disappeared by now; but he did it gingerly, without hurting the window pane. The last time he had taken the train to the city, in the middle of winter, to see the doctor, they had accompanied him and turned away the minute the wheels started roll-ing. . .behind the closed door he couldn't have waved back at them, even if the thought of waving had occurred to them. . .or they would not have seen it, had he waved, so why bother. So what, they simply didn't think of it, good Lord, a ride into town, when they'd be seeing each other in the evening as usual, and the doctor wouldn't bite his head off. . . .

Brämi waited. . .he was crazy enough, at this moment, to wait for nothing but the waving that had not been waved at the station. And as he admitted this to himself, he opened his eyes a little and *saw*; saw not the land any longer but a face reflected in the window, the smudged face of a child, with a pink, smoking stick of candy in his mouth. His face: what a delusion to believe that he ever had a different one. He lowered his eyes. Just a moment, he thought. Just a moment, I must let this waiting die. It was the wrong wish. Now I no longer have a wish, I've survived it.

Now he had time. He took a step back into the room; it was a step of courtesy, the kind that allows everything else to go before, all who wanted to go and who had already gone. He opened his eyes, the wisp of smoke at this mouth wafted to one side. The window no longer mirrored, it framed a compact, random piece of land without a sky. Not a soul could be seen in it now. He fastened his eyes on the small stretch of willows which remained in the picture, on the mere hint of a softness, of a submerging of land into land, which had the shape of a crumbly, dead-end furrow; and he was waiting, effortlessly leaning against the edge of

the bed, for nothing any longer. Now he was just there—
THERE!

The explosion had blown off the upper front of the house,
had uncovered part of the roof, scattering the tiles as far as
half a mile, according to the people who live on the farm
now. They were taking it for granted—and my matter-of-
fact attitude reassured them—that my kinship to Brämi
was distant enough to allow them to speak of his end
without false piety. "They had to scrape him off the
walls," said the farmer, a man who had attended an agricultural college and who looked more like a young con-
tractor who is close to his native soil. Nor is his wife what
older people would consider a typical Oberland farmer's
wife. She is from the Bern region, has remained loyal to
her dialect, and often reads sophisticated books. Perhaps
they find it embarrassing, to have taken over a legacy to
which they are not bound by family ties, but not too
embarrassing. Seen next to old photographs, the property
isn't recognizable; it has an addition on one side—the new
living room is quite suburban, with a TV set and an open
fireplace—and has been enlarged by farm buildings
designed according to the most advanced principles of
agricultural efficiency. The daughters left soon after, they
said, the woman remarried, an innkeeper from the March
region; she sold the farm, the young agronomist said. We're
already the third owners. I nodded absent-mindedly, for it
struck me for the first time that I'd never taken the trouble
to look for Brämi's descendants, my distant cousins; evidently my mother hadn't done so either. Their name can
no longer be Rüesch, and I think that if they're still alive,
they would not want to be sought and reminded of the
tragedy.

You know, the young woman said, I think people in
those days didn't communicate. They held back on every-

thing, trying to come to grips with things on their own, but they didn't know how. They talked a lot about being neighborly, but neighbors were good only for practical emergencies. I believe that a kind of civil war used to go on in most houses, and it wore people thin. It seems to me that our parents—and suddenly she was talking about her own parents—lived only by their guilt feelings, and that was something they couldn't do. And then they were surprised when everything suddenly went to pieces. I nodded at these words which surely contained some truth and might be helpful toward a different, easier life, but this isn't granted to everyone, not even today, not even under urban conditions. In this respect some people are still—perhaps more so today—living in the backwoods, so to speak. "Yes, they used to make a mountain out of every molehill," added the young farmer, and I suddenly wasn't so sure if he had understood his wife, and if in the long run things would be all right between those two. But the young woman only said that one just had to try to relate to others, and that everything depended on being positive, on seeing the positive side of things.

Today I know that the tremendous bang, which my mother kept from me, had not been allowed in her life. I understand very well why she refuses to consider Brämi's death a disgrace, because disgrace has a very different look. Perhaps I would never have been born if my mother had found the strength to live for her own happiness. And yet I know that the explosion which was Brämi's death should have happened in her life, should have happened, whatever the price. If it is true that she avoided discord for my sake, then I want, at least, to name this price. I cannot pay it. For me the time of great tones and sounds is gone.

But I will name it by name, unyielding and useful on this point alone. For it is this point, the point of absolute honesty, around which the earth must be turned if that for which it was created is to be fulfilled.

# GRANDFATHER'S LITTLE PLEASURE

Grandfather doesn't like talking about his visit to the brothel, but whenever we ask him nicely he gives in. He is the sturdiest in our family. When, on some mornings, we all stay in bed a little longer, he sits down at our bedside, dressed in his spotless uniform from the '70s. Tell us, we then say. He is living with us; in return he tells something. We pay close attention every time whether the story stays the same. The following is a summary of all the other stories which Grandfather, sitting at our bedside, has told us about his visit to the brothel.

One morning during his middle years, Grandfather, carrying his sample case with five pieces of artificial turf, arrived at the faraway railroad junction of Njesa.

It was 10:30 A.M.; the meeting with the president of the Athletic Club was not to take place until 3:00 P.M.

A sizable market had opened up around Njesa, sur‐ rounded by wooden churches and junipers. Grandfather had taken the sleeper car in the Forest–Heath–Express to be the first traveling salesman who would acquaint the Njesa district — which pervaded even the passing trains with the sweet smell of its lilacs — with artificial turf. What grew here, even on the athletic fields, was still the old, worn down and delicate green.

But when he stood there, at 10:30 and also at 10:35 A.M. in the square outside the Njesa railroad station, where the sun was already casting harsh shadows, all he could think of — looking up and down the high–storied houses — was that it was still too early for lunch. His mouth dry, he had stood there, facing the dirt–colored vagueness of Njesa, searching in vain for an appetite. All of a sudden he did not feel like entering a town where the cuisine, by and large, was still brutish.

Pot roast with sauce Remoulade! We call from the bed. In short, Grandfather had stepped from the station into the open, without a definite goal; the sample case weighed so little that he didn't resist the idea of a walk; so he crossed onto the shady side of the street and avoiding the open square he let himself be led by the first best row of houses. It ran parallel to the tracks, in the direction from which his train had come. The sidewalk was so narrow that he was unable to take a good look at the shadowy buildings he almost brushed with his shoulder. However, he had the impression of entering a district where only manual services of the rougher or noisier kind were located: auto repair shops where wind–driven ventilators turned lazily in the still air, a brewery with rundown, badly paved ramps, warehouses for tubeless tires and things of that sort, also barracks for foreign laborers, partially boarded up.

Go on, Grandfather, we say.

And always the trains in the corner of his left eye, clumsily maneuvering back and forth, rumbling into each other under drawn out whistles, while the heat was sizzling over the tracks. Gradually the landscape of tracks became larger and bleaker, and on his side too there were fewer buildings, only sheds by now, except for one single high structure, displaying on its blind wall a cocoa advertise—ment which, flashing white teeth, enhanced the sense of isolation.

A cocoa ad! we laugh.

Naturally, under the circumstances the sunny intervals between the shadows became more and more spacious, and to the same extent also the sky which in its glare seemed almost dark to the eyes.

Boy, does he keep us in suspense, we say, huddling in our blankets. Now he has begun to age, says Grandfather, but even then he wasn't all that young anymore. That's why all of a sudden he was aware of his legs and the sweat on his forehead; so he decided to turn back at the single house with the cocoa advertisement. One should always set oneself a goal in life. At the house he stopped for a moment to put his decision into practice, or to put it more simply: to turn around. From the front it was a house in the style of French apartment blocks which in turn were mod—elled—however faintly—on French chateaux (aha! we say at this point), with a gray faceted roof uncommon in this area, hidden until now by the billboard; and now too you could see the scaffolding holding up the board from the attic windows. There were no shutters, however; instead the mostly broken window frames and sills had a layer of pink paint over older yellow. These traces of elegance had an effect curiously enhanced by the isolated location of the house; part of the effect was also a faded brown sign on the facade, between the second and third floor, obviously outdated, naming in gothic script a certain Hartmuth Müller, Coal. He had to step back a few feet in order to decipher it, which the wide, even endless sidewalk now permitted. The strangely remote thundering of the trains at his back, the accelerating thumps of a steam locomotive unleashing themselves into the distance, the strain of having to squint into the sun, and the sudden weight of the sample case drove him back into the shade where he was going to turn back; and in this moment, an old doorman materialized, detached himself from the shade and extending his arm politely, left him no choice but to enter.

Here it comes, we say, stuffing our fists into our mouths.

The hall he entered, Grandfather goes on, remained empty for several seconds. Only the sensation of having chanced into some kind of hospital made the seconds pass, and probably the coolness too—emitted by the pastel walls and doors, imitation wallpaper and wood: emitted breathlessly, so to speak, because plastic doesn't breathe. He saw door upon door, as in a pidgeon coop, a morgue or a nursery school; something hopelessly quaint lay in the air, reminding him of nothing, nothing at all, at best perhaps of an unknown loss.

But then a scantily dressed girl stepped up to him with an accommodating smile; opened her lips as if about to speak when a second female figure moved into position, pushing her back a little; she seemed dressed for an old-fashioned ball and looked up to him with her ceremoniously painted face. He turned to her and asked with a faint smile if one could get something to drink there, that he really had no other desires but to spend a quiet hour in *intelligent* company. With the same smile and a glance at his sample case, the lady assured him that every client could do as he pleased, but that they were not permitted to serve alcoholic beverages. As for a bright little head, and she turned to the scantily dressed girl, he would certainly get his money's worth with this one, and by way of suggestion freed the space between them. He then asked what his expenses might be and got the answer: this would be between him and the girl. He repeated that he was looking only for a quiet chat and something to drink, but at that point the lady with the harshly painted face had already turned away and he actually found himself following the girl up the first steps of the staircase. What he could make out from her face was neither unpleasant nor enticing, a reminder of no one he'd ever known, at best perhaps the wife of an old friend whom he hadn't seen in years; there had not been a particular bond between him and this woman either, not even some special conversation. He climbed stair after stair, following the girl, and the distance between them increased. The staircase, too, was obviously washable, surfaces joined together without a speck of dust and, although existing in space, with no depth at all. He kept climbing after the girl in her red, ribbon-trimmed panties and brassiere, through pure *surfaces* and noticed suddenly that in these non-spaces there wasn't a glimmer of daylight. The bright lightbulbs in their decorative wire cages located at regular intervals on the staircase ceiling, smoothed away all edges. The gauze curtains which he had seen from the outside were presumably draped boards. He did feel a rise in temperature now, which was utterly different from the warmth outside; its faint oily smell took on a hint of cologne as they were climbing higher and higher—and the house seemed infinitely higher on the inside than on the outside; it was a stale warmth, reminding him of hard times. And finally the girl, calling him "honey," opened a pink door in a light green corner, letting him enter into a really heavy warmth. She then, as on command, sat down on a chair by the wall, tapped a cigarette from her pack, lit it, while he remained standing there, not sure where to sit down.

Now we listen to Grandfather, holding our breath. He said that in this small room with artificial—but not unfriendly—lights, there had been a bed taking up the corner opposite the door; it had some kind of wooden frame around it on which souvenirs were crowded together, just like in a shooting gallery at some country fair. The bed itself did not seem to be made for use or even rest; it was barricaded, so to speak, by several heavy woollen blankets and secured by an enormous Bambi.

A Bambi? We ask.

A deer, says Grandfather.

Oh, a deer, we say and don't understand a word.

The thought alone of doing anything having to do with that bed required an effort. Behind the headboard the frame continued toward the door, extending into the flat top of a slightly higher cabinet, where two white plastic molds with flat eye sockets were standing, probably for the use of wigs. Above this cabinet hung a framed regulation listing an exit plan in case of fire. Behind the door a radiator completed the arrangement. Hard at the foot of the bed stood a table covered with a brown, fringed table-cloth; a few bright-colored magazines were on top, one of them called *The Courier*. The girl sat at the far end of the table, smoking hastily. Just opposite the girl, next to the door, stood a low shelf stuffed with jars, tubes and bottles. The larger spray cans on the top shelf were reflected in a mirror, which however did not take in all their bright colors; and yet it was neither tinted nor dusty. Next to this, by the closed window, diagonally across from the bed, was a cot with a raised headrest; its end was wrapped in pale plastic, evidently to protect against shoe marks; on the middle section of the cot lay a terry towel folded lengthwise.

He ought to have seen the house, said the girl, before the present owner had taken over and set in order. A sleazy joint it was, one to be ashamed of. But that was before her time.

He, Grandfather, had nodded, still looking for a suitable seat. One thing was clear: any kind of settling down in this room would seem an overture to certain acts. To keep at least some kind of company with the girl there at the table, he had to use the edge of the bed; of course he had no room for his legs under the table but had to stretch them, one over the other, straight out into the little room. Only then did he put down his sample case. Now he was sitting with the girl at the same wall after all; if he had leaned back, Grandfather said, he would have upset the souvenirs on the frame. He repeated his request for something to drink, whereupon she repeated the word "honey" or "hon" and left the room very quickly. After a few minutes she put a glass in front of him, holding her cigarette in the same hand, and standing in the half open door, she opened the small bottle of lemonade by prying it with both hands against the door lock, squinting over the cigarette dangling from her mouth. After she had poured, Grandfather wondered if it was wise to drink from the glass. But later on he did anyhow. She had not brought a glass for herself. Then, as on the stairs when he had said it too softly, he asked her not to call him "honey." He shouldn't be upset, she said, it came naturally with her job. Later on she added that that kind of talk hadn't been easy for her in the beginning, but since she was much in demand, it had become a habit, more or less. Every now and then Grandfather would bring the glass to his lips without actually touching it; and so some of its contents dripped down on his trousers. A look at the many photographs of children on the bed frame provided the opportunity to ask about her family. As it turned out, the little girl was not *her* as a child but her *daughter*, now five years old. All the photographs portrayed the same child in different years. But in a color photo he also recognized her, leaning against the fender of a car, one arm around the driver who, in turn, was holding on to the steering wheel with both hands. He was light blond, smiling a vague but pleasant smile, as one does in photographs. And there was the third figure of a mutual friend, slightly cut off by the margin.

To look at the pictures he had to get up again, which was no trouble since one did not sink down into the bed.

He walked about the room a little, asked permission to guess her age and, as it turned out, overestimated by three years.

But she didn't seem to mind. When asked about her background, she said she had been born in this city and grown up in a part of town beyond the railroad station and, in reply to another question—that she had been working here for the last two years. It hadn't been easy to find an opening, the owner was choosy—she was a studied woman— and the city was very particular about the good reputation of the candidates. In another two years she said, she hoped to have saved enough money for her own beauty parlor, said Grandfather. At that moment a terrible scream was heard throughout the house. In response to the raised eyebrows of our grandfather, still pacing aimlessly, the girl explained that the screaming woman was the oldest in the house, about forty-five already. She wasn't quite right in the head and sadly unable to do any other work. And yet she owned two luxuriously furnished apartments with many appliances—she hardly knew how to use any of them—she couldn't even fry an egg. Whenever the phone rang she was so scared she'd switch off the TV and all lights, hoping this way she would be less visible to the caller on the phone. Even after the phone stopped ringing she would sit in the dark for quite some time, just to be sure.

Ho ho, we say, and Grandfather thinks we're laughing.

It wasn't funny at all, he says, and he asked the girl if it wouldn't be detrimental to her beauty shop if people in town knew that she had worked here? He wouldn't believe, she replied, how few people knew about it. Except for her parents and her boyfriend, only her sister; and they had more or less resigned themselves to the fact. Grandfather asked if she had many out-of-town clients—Americans, for example?—and she replied that that wasn't the case, not really. Here he sensed a contradiction but tactfully refrained from pointing it out. As he was reading the brothel regulations on the wall which listed the details of permissible intercourse in this establishment, as well as the girls' fees and their responsibilities in compliance with the health authorities, he was reminded of a contemporary artist who had illustrated a similar document from another city with drawings which were more hilarious than risqué. To direct their conversation onto a more personal level—and he felt some obligation to do so since her nervous smoking and cross-legged position on the chair began to make him feel uncomfortable—he asked her if she could give him some advice in a private matter.

Is this really true, Grandfather? all of us laugh.

Gentleman of the old school that he is, Grandfather never reacts at this point but continues more or less like this: the girl replied without the slightest hesitation that he had picked the wrong person for his question. She had never experienced it herself, neither with her boyfriend nor at any other time. She sometimes toyed with the thought of seeing a doctor, but it cost too much; besides, she wasn't missing anything and didn't see why she ought to have it. She was a person with a mind of her own. That she had a mind of her own she repeated more than once that morning, but she also admitted that there were some in this house who'd experience it now and then. They would say: if you're enjoying it, why not let yourself go — but they were a minority here. Did it bother her just to chat with him for a while, Grandfather then asked and she replied, no, not at all.

When he lay down beside her cradling her wig-covered head like a barren shrub in his arms, she stroked his back a few times which made him think of someone writing, without looking, on a board, with the tiniest piece of chalk in such a way, that the fingernails too grated along a little.

Hold it, we say. Haven't you left out something here?

We say this every time but never succeed in closing the gap in his memory. Not at all, he says every time; he had most certainly not left out anything, and he fills his pipe, blushing in the reflection of the match.

There are passages which you have suppressed, we say. Grandfather, it is a love story.

Oh, yes indeed, he did love us, Grandfather says, drawing like mad on his pipe.

All right, Grandfather, we say sternly through all the smoke. Up to this point you have been precise, almost punctilious, Grandfather, but now you're beginning to slip. We have information about cocoa advertisements in your time; even railroad stations can be imagined if need be; and artificial turf we have seen for ourselves. However, we are left in the dark about vast areas of private experience in your time; and don't forget: you are a source.

Grandfather begins to weep.

You can't fool us, Grandfather, we say. With all due respect to your memories, our curiosity, which is scientific, is at stake. There used to be certain copulation techniques, and you knew them, too. So out with it.

Grandfather tries hard to weep silently, but he doesn't fool us, the old man.

Today no peanut butter, tomorrow no TV special, we say. We too have our means.

Grandfather dries his tears. He had not left out anything then, he says. He tried to move, to reach that body bound only with two thin chains, one around her neck, the other around her hips, with a tinkling medallion on it.

A medallion, Grandfather? we ask, for inconspicuous finds often lead to the discovery of entire civilizations.

With a head on it, says Grandfather, there was the head of an emperor on the medallion.

Impossible, we say, the girl could not have been that old.

Grandfather says that he asked her if she was a Catholic, but she denied it vehemently.

Catholic or not, we say, where did you have your face, Grandfather?

Near her ear, says Grandfather.

Contradiction! contradiction! we cry. If you had your face near her ear, you could not have seen the medallion, Grandfather, since it was dangling from her hips—your so-called emperor was playing with her pubic hair, yes or no? We know pubic hair from the dictionary.

He could *feel* the medallion, Grandfather said—in those days one's belly was still sensitive. Besides, in the meantime he had had plenty of chances to look at it.

In the meantime? We act surprised. Well now, this is the first time we hear about it. What happened to this "meantime," Grandfather?

He had asked himself that question too; and that we could no longer understand it, says Grandfather, "because you are nothing but little colored blocks, hard little blocks in your little beds." That's how direct our grandfather can become when he feels cornered. You can hear his pipe snort.

Well, Grandfather, you tried to move the girl, we say magnanimously, because his opinion of us doesn't matter. And then?

Grandfather picks up his thread: the girl quivered all the time, it was a constant undercurrent quiver, apparently of a nervous nature, because it could neither be suppressed nor increased. It communicated itself much like shivering, as the result of a tense hopelessness or of some expectation all jammed up somewhere, and not even tact would lossen it again.

And there Grandfather goes again, weeping, and doesn't even take his pipe out of his mouth.

Tut, tut, Grandfather, we cluck, you and your tact, when you have no need for it.

That was precisely it, Grandfather swallows, he had no need for it, there had been no need for him to be there, and that was the reason he had been unable to rescue — better, tear away this girl who quivered so unnaturally. She, at least, had a beauty shop to show for herself, but he? Apart from a few pieces of artificial turf nothing but the fading wish to turn back at this house. Some heat over the railroad tracks wasn't good enough a reason. Nothing but coincidence had weighed on him when he entered there, in short, he had not felt any love, and therefore had no business being there and screwing.

That was quite a word, we cry, we found it in the dictionary, go on now, Grandfather, let's have it, we say, clapping our hands rhythmically to get Grandfather going; we finally want to see him squirm, the noble old gentleman. But he remains silent, at best he nods a little keeping time to our clapping, after all, he doesn't want to ruin our fun. He is biding his time until we get tired; we tire quickly, and he knows it. Even if we wanted to, we cannot deny him the peanut butter, because he is the one who brings it to our bedside — we have no one else. On the way he can lick his fingers as much as he likes. That is the misery of our age — it is still dependent on the older generation. But he lets us feel this on rare occasions only, he is still a gentleman. It is only when he tells a story that he does whatever he wants with us.

There were no "passages" in his story, he says. If we wanted "passages," we should go look them up in our dirty old books.

First of all, they are your books, Grandfather, we say; secondly, you lock them up wherever possible and thirdly, "passages" there are quite general, and love was something special in those days. You say so yourself, Grandfather, we say.

No, it wasn't anything special, Grandfather says, and no power of persuasion would prove the contrary. The girl kept answering with the same stubborn presence of mind, fixing her eyes firmly on the ceiling. At one time he touched her and tried to judge her weight, again too much, and again she didn't take offense, no offense at all; fat doesn't weigh much, she had said. And then, all of a sudden, as if he had put a coin into some slot machine, she had started wiggling about —

You see, Grandfather! we are triumphant; warm, Grandfather, press on, Grandfather!

—but then he had slapped her hand immediately and we never found out where she had her hand at that moment. Then she put her arms behind her head to prove to him that she had not wanted to set up a trap—that was another vague expression in Grandfather's report. His touchiness, however, prevented him from appreciating this little beauty of a moral gesture. Instead he was searching for her ear, to speak to it, first with his lips, then with his teeth. All he had wanted to do was *play*, Grandfather blurted out.

Now you have us, we say maliciously, little, hard, colored blocks.

That's true, Grandfather says sadly.

We are scientists and not inhuman, therefore we ask: what did you want to say into the girl's ear?

Nothing, Grandfather says, blushing again. Something kind, perhaps, about her little daughter, something about the weather in Njesa. But she would not be moved by him. Then, as he said earlier, he had grasped her ear with his teeth.

And then? we ask, because it is a beautiful passage every time.

Grandfather screams, losing his control altogether, but he can't get rid of us that easily.

It's all in our dictionary, we say, we want to know what it was like in reality.

Reality, always reality, Grandfather complains; reality in those days was beginning to come undone; you could tell, because children like us were born—*anaemic* creatures—and had multiplied by leaps and bounds. In the old days, tremendous efforts were made in the service of love, he says, entire generations of youth melted away over it. Decent people then still refused to believe that the human condition "was curable in one point alone." But in

Grandfather's young manhood, certain varieties of feelings were already lost, for which a need was felt much later on, and then, quite naturally, one stopped missing them.

Traces of elements, we nod.

You acted only out of some undefined need, visited a brothel, for example, and now there were but a few left— period pieces, so to speak, reminding of a time when love had been something special. But he must be boring us, Grandfather says at this point in his story, which he elaborates more forcefully on some occasions than on others.

It doesn't matter, Grandfather, we say. Collect yourself. What did you do with the girl's ear?

He returned it, says Grandfather, and by and by finds his way back into his story; we let him, there's nothing more to be gotten out of him. At first it felt as if a sign of life might be drawn from this ear, she was even whispering now: no, please, no, and again: no, dammit. That sounded genuine, but only because he was really beginning to annoy her and she spitefully tossed her head back and forth. As if this ear with all the horse hair around it had been all that much fun. He, however, happy at last to see a reaction without wanting to know where it would lead and whether it was a reaction at all and not a struggle against it—presumably a struggle become routine long ago; after all, what hopes could she possibly set in him who had chanced into this place by coincidence, and most likely she had made it one of the rules of her life not to understand any signs for hope—where was he?

You, however, we said. He knows the words but we are good in grammer.

That's right, he, however, had clung for a few moments to this flesh numbed in its hopelessness, as if life could still be engendered here or its loss be made up.

Orgasm? We ask at this point.

Why not, says Grandfather, and doesn't blush any-more. It had no longer any significance.

Tell the rest, Grandfather, we say. We know him— nothing more to be squeezed out of him.

Although he was lying on top, he goes on, the impression therefore misleading, her body under and away from him had closed into a stubborn ball denying him all support, unyielding; in order not to slide off, he had to support his weight with his arms. In this position, but bent over, he had tried to fill her ear with a sound gentle enough not to be shaken out immediately. But, he says, she pressed her ear too into the ball her flesh had formed against him. So then he let go, screaming the rest into her breasts; those breasts were of an exhausted pointedness, which reminded him of home, perhaps of something knit-ted by his mother. With those breasts the girl's body seemed strangely *clothed*, however poorly, as if something here had to be treated with great care. When he finally raised himself on his arms to give her a chance to uncurl, an absolutely unequivocal gesture, she uttered a sigh of relief and, without giving him so much as a glance she repeated—that's the way she was, a person with a mind of her own. Honey, she added after a pause. And: Sorry.

Then they got right up, and there was no further need for a gratuitous gesture.

From the cot?

From the cot.

What a pity, we say. Actually we don't like such stories at all—as stories, that is; and as documentaries they remain too skimpy.

While he dressed slowly Grandfather watched as she first sprayed her private parts, then dried off with a reso-lute rub of the towel. The domestic appeal of this gesture prompted him once again — pushing his arms through his shirt sleeves, his shirt front still unbuttoned — to stroke her stiff, almost glazed hair. Honey, she said and no longer apologized for it. While he gave a look at his watch — almost noon — he asked her if she had to accommodate every client. On principle, every client, she answered, unless he was dirty or drunk, but Turks and Italians were, on principle, not permitted to undress completely. He opened his wallet asking how much he owned — 250 — which she tucked away in a small strong box on her bedframe. This box she had left open, by the way, during the two times she had left the room. He then took his sample case by the handle, it felt light once again. Despite his protest, says Grandfather, she accompanied him down all the stairs to the exit; it was customary in this house to do so, she explained. As he let her go ahead, he was aware for the last time of the undefined firmness of her flesh, constricted by tight-fitting panties and brassiere. The owner no longer showed herself — evidently a sign that no one was interested in his return.

You must be mistaken there, Grandfather, we say, but he doesn't want comfort.

He went in, says Grandfather, because twenty years earlier, as a youth, he had toyed with the idea; almost forty by this time, he could finally accept the fact that he had not entered before. In the open door he wondered if he should say goodbye to the girl with a bow, and he did.

And at this very moment the clock struck twelve. Twelve o'clock noon.

Huh, we say and give a frightened scream.

So that's the way it went in the brothels, we say.

No, says Grandfather, that's the way it went with me, and that was probably my fault.

And what about the artificial turf, Grandfather, we

ask, and Njesa? and the athletic club?

Grandfather remains silent. Once he has finished his story or thinks he has, he wants no part of the artificial turf, he rolls it out only for the first move of that game. What was this eternal turf on which the Njesa Soccer Club won or lost, compared with the 0:0 score in the house with the cocoa advertisement, near the tracks and close to noon. It had been a long time ago, it had been nothing, or almost nothing, but something in itself.

We are fond of our grandfather. He is still capable of blushing, he is not of our time. But he still knows how to tell a story, he is still a storyteller.

# DINNERTIME

"How wonderful! How nice!" comes a hoarse but instantly recognizable voice from upstairs as someone, the uncle from America, overtaxing himself, hastily negotiates the descent, always dragging his rear foot before moving on with the first. Peter sits off to the side, hidden under this staircase at an odd angle; he should remain here, the young lady told him before going upstairs to prepare the uncle for his visit; if the uncle saw him right away, standing at the foot of the stairs, he might come down precipitously and hurt himself or else not come down at all; there was no way of knowing.

Therefore Peter is careful not to react to the periodic "How wonderful! How nice!" but listens instead from his little upholstered chair to this descent which sounds so forceful on the flimsy stairs. He sees the hand of a man as it jerks clumsily down the banister, then holds on to it again, trembling; behind, without pressing on the wood,

sallow hand of a woman. "How wonderful! How nice!"
Peter hears now almost next to his ear; probably now he
can stand up. And loosening up his shoulders and putting
on a smile he positions himself at the bottom of the stairs,
looking up into the shrunken face of his uncle from
America which comes within arm's reach, without a sign of
recognition, without a change in expression.

Peter nods, steps back a little, and stretches out his arm
toward the uncle. The uncle grasps this arm and shakes it
vigorously without leaning on it. But he really needs
support until he reaches the bottom of the stairs. Once
more Peter steps aside, letting him touch ground, surprised
at the delicate care with which the uncle releases his arm.
Even stooped the uncle is tall. Here they remain standing
until the young lady has moved between them, clearing
space—and there isn't much space in this house—for a
small ceremonial greeting. But the moment has passed,
they have already touched each other, and so remain
standing, and it seems as if the uncle wants to catch a
glimpse, over Peter's shoulder, of another visitor, the real
one.

"But this is Peter," says the young lady, "Peter! Peter
has come from Switzerland, imagine."

"Aha, ah, oh yes," the uncle says, straightening himself up, up on his toes, not looking at Peter. "How wonderful, very nice. I thank you, sir."

"I am here on a business trip," says Peter, "and so I
wanted to look in—"

But the uncle pays no attention. He has begun whispering to the young lady.

"Yes, yes," the young lady says aloud. "It doesn't
matter, not at all. It doesn't bother you if he isn't shaved,
does it."

"Of course not!" Peter says. "It is more informal this way."

"Peter would like to take you on a ride," the young lady says. "Imagine. To Utica."

"Have I been there before?" the uncle asks. "I haven't been there yet," he says. "I believe, I haven't yet been there."

"You have been there a thousand times, Uncle," says Peter. "Utica! That's where you always had your office."

"Again the uncle whispers into the young lady's ear. "No! no!" the young lady says firmly.

Quizzically the uncle turns his face to Peter; it is a glance from many years ago; only the eyes have become wider—or more hollow—and somewhat moist; after one of these mysteriously firm glances they drift off to the side again.

"Oui," the uncle says, "On fait des voyages maintenant. Beaucoup. Pas mal de voyages. A Paris, ah oui. Les gens font des voyages maintenant."

"You can talk Swiss German to Peter, I don't mind a bit," says the young lady. She has an evenly mild tone, is probably not all that young, her skin seems mealy from powdering, her hair is grayish blond, ageless.

"Ah oui, oui," the uncle says and his French becomes even hastier, as if he were taking an exam; in quick succession he names several French tourist spots, following each of them with a brief deprecating clearing of his throat.

"Father sends his regards," Peter says.

"It is very kind of you, sir," says the uncle from America, "very kind of you to say so."

Peter tries again. "From Erich, greetings from Erich," he says. "Oh!" says the uncle and the alert smile of a man who used to be at ease with people flits across his face.

"Eric!" He gives the name an English pronunciation, will not be deterred from English.

"You know him?"

"But Mr. Shallenberger," says the young lady, "Erich is Peter's father."

"So you also know Peter?" asks the uncle from America, pinching his eyes shut.

"I think, we'll drive to Utica now, Mr. Shallenberger, and eat something nice," the young lady says. "You'll have a lot to say to each other, you and your nephew."

"I haven't been there before, no," the uncle says again very plesantly, "I have kept you waiting too long. My apologies." He touches the back of his pants. "It can be washed again. Now I remember."

"It is not as it was in Fir Lodge," says the young lady, "is it, Mr. Shallenberger? Here we have a big garden, and a bath, and a room of our own, and television. Cherokee Manor is not like Fir Lodge."

Peter takes his uncle by his free arm, they walk outside onto the graveled esplanade which is lined by maples, shocking pink, yellow and orange like a spring display in a department store.

"Do you watch television, Uncle?" Peter asks; talking comes more easily when you're walking, it becomes less important. But the uncle stops short.

"Whom?" asks the uncle. "No, I don't see him often, not at all. Definitely not." As he walks on he holds his hand out to Peter and presses it briefly.

Out in the open the uncle is even more stooped as he proceeds with careful exploring steps as if he didn't trust the ground but his companions ought not to notice.

"He doesn't always understand the words," says the young lady. "But then he understands the meaning after all. It just takes patience."

"What I mean is," Peter says and, he has to slow down his step, chafing against the deep gravel, "do you like watching television?"

"I don't see him, certainly not," says the uncle. "Or" — and he stops again turning to the young woman — "weren't there people? A lot of people?" And with a half turn to Peter, "That's right, there were people there, I remember."

"All of us here are very fond of him," the young lady says. "He is still such a gentlemen."

"Once upon a time," the uncle says with a faint wink. They have arrived at Peter's rented car, but Peter must let his uncle have his say before asking him to get in. The uncle holds the rear door for the young lady, but when she asks him to get in before her, he obeys hastily, first bumping his shoulder, then his head.

"Pas de quoi, Mademoiselle," he says. "C'est comme toujours. Vous me connaissez."

While they are following the signs to Utica, Peter at the wheel, the other two in the back, the uncle whispers incessantly to the young lady. He probably thinks that he is being abducted, that Peter is some new kind of doctor expecting things from him that cannot be fulfilled.

Peter finds it easier than on the way over to ignore the bright-colored clumps of trees and to keep his eyes on the road. Nevertheless he drives very slowly, lets others pass him; his own grip on the steering wheel strikes him as pretentious.

In Utica they pass the office building where the uncle used to work. A red brick house, New England style; sunlight has left the lower stories, the white window cornices shine as if it were already night. Forty years of his life, but the uncle gives no sign of recognition.

"Remember? In your car I took my first ride, after the

war. You had brought it with you to Europe. A Studebaker." In the middle of traffic Peter turns to face his uncle who is laughing without a sound, as if over a good joke. "Yes, a Studebaker," he says. "That is very kind of you, sir."

The restaurant where, at Peter's request, the young lady has reserved a table, is not one of the better ones and almost empty, only the loudspeakers allow some life to trickle into the room. It is actually just the cafeteria of a movie house; the uncle whispers to the young lady that he needs to go to the bathroom. After a wink back and forth it is Peter who accompanies his uncle outside, through the empty vestibule. The layout is obscure, but the uncle peacefully goes along with Peter's meanderings through several corridors. Finally it turns out that one gets to the toilets only through the projection room. The uncle stops once behind the dimly lit rows of seats and says, "I have never been here. No. But it is beautiful too." And as Peter nods the uncle puts a hand on his arm. "You come from Switzerland, bien sûr?" he asks. "Mais oui, mais oui. Here it is not like Switzerland. Not everything. Don't you think so?"

Peter turns around. "Would you like to return to Switzerland, Uncle?" he asks.

"Ah, Switzerland," the uncle says, for the first time in Swiss dialect. "La Suisse. I have been there too."

"Of course you have been there," Peter says, "even after I had been born. That's where you grew up. In Elgg."

"Elgg!" The uncle laughs. Then he seems to inspect the velvet curtain; a piece of screen is glaring through its gap. "What a long way to school we had," he says. "Even in winter. It was too much for children. Far too long."

"I bring you regards. From Erich, my father. Your brother."

"Yes, Erich, that one," the uncle says. "Do you know him, sir?"

"I live in Winterthur," Peter says after a while.

"Winterthur! You know it?"

"Not as well as you, Uncle, that's where you attended the College of Engineering."

"You know all that," the uncle says. "So you know that too. It is very kind of you to take the trouble, sir."

"Come," Peter says. "The young lady is waiting for us." As he takes the uncle by the arm, the old man, almost eagerly, slips into his grasp; he's snuggling up, Peter is thinking. "Look, over there," Peter says. "I'll wait."

He watches as the uncle attempts to close the swinging toilet door behind him. In the past, every three months the uncle would send from America a check which at the exchange rate yielded a fabulous sum for Peter's family— his mother had died when he was seven years old. A three-digit number to be multiplied by almost five! And during his first visit to Switzerland after the war, this uncle had bought Peter a wristwatch and impressed him with the American lilt of his almost forgotten native dialect. After the uncle's every visit, Peter for some time would pronounce the "ja –a" with the drawl of an American, and was made fun of in school. But he remained loyal to the tic, for a few weeks; it made the uncle with his power from overseas somewhat less absent.

He appears again in the door and looks around.

"Ah," he says as Peter takes two steps toward him.

"You are still open, Uncle," Peter says. The uncle jerks his head a little and looks at Peter as if something very funny had happened, while his fingers frantically arrange the buttons on his pants; it doesn't work. Then the uncle turns halfway and, stooping a little, labors intently, by himself.

On the way back through the theater the uncle says again in English, "That's the way it is, alas." Then he touches his jacket with both thumbs. "Do you like it? Very sturdy. Made to last," he says, rubbing the lapels between thumb and index finger. His face shines with anxious pleasure. "I am glad," the uncle says. "Look at the pockets, sir." He opens his jacket. "Here, and here, and here," he says.

"Please come," Peter says.

"It doesn't matter, does it," the uncle says confidentially.

"It doesn't matter, Uncle," Peter says. "Are you a little bit hungry?"

"Am I hungry?" asks the uncle and stops. "A little hungry? Many thanks."

One didn't have to reserve a table in this empty room. The young lady is putting on lipstick. She continues as the uncle and Peter sit down. With a movement of the head she indicates the menu on the table. "Something easy to digest for him," she says, pinching her lips.

"A steak perhaps." And clears away her tools, snapping shut the lock of her small purse.

"I don't have my glasses with me," the uncle says and picks up the menu without looking at it.

"Yes, he is allowed to have his glasses again," the young lady says.

"There is a curry dish," says Peter after a look at the menu.

"Not for him," the young lady says.

"What would you like to eat, Uncle?" Peter asks. "You choose whatever you like."

"Would I like to?" the uncle asks turning to the young lady. "What would I like to eat?"

"You would probably enjoy a well-done steak," the young lady says. The waitress has approached the table; first she looks at the uncle who is fidgeting, then she becomes particularly friendly. "We have good baked fish today," she says.

"Too fatty," the young lady says. "Give him a steak, but well done."

Peter looks at the uncle but the uncle doesn't say anything. Under these circumstances Peter also orders a steak; the young lady ponders for a long time before she reconsiders the fish, for herself.

After the waitress has left, a silence spreads which the uncle finds disturbing; again and again he fingers the cloth of his suit. "You have a beautiful suit, Mr. Shallenberger," the young lady says. "You look twenty years younger in it." And to Peter in the same tone, "He can't believe he has a suit again, a fountain pen and a watch. At Fir Lodge they had only these institutional clothes. One has to understand why."

The uncle slips off his watch and puts it on the table. "We still have some time, don't we still have some time?" he asks the young lady.

"And how!" Peter says. "Today we do precisely what you'd like, Uncle." The Uncle looks at Peter, nods shyly; then, with the chivalry of a man who at one time had been at home in the world, he turns to his escort and asks, "What would you like me to do? I have never been here. Have I been here before?"

"But of course you have been here," the young lady says. "You know every tree here, every house." She gives Peter a firm smile.

"And your nephew has an invitation for you, he wants to treat you to something."

The uncle stares at his watch; then he pulls it over his wrist again, straightens his cuff, quickly looking around the large room.

"You gave me a watch, right after the war, when you came over for the first time," Peter says. "Remember? A watch with a black face. It had been ordered by the German air force. But when the war was over, it had to be sold in Switzerland. But for me it was still a pilot's watch. I was very proud of it. And it lasted fifteen years. Now it no longer works, but I still treasure it."

"So," the uncle says. "It is very kind of you, sir."

"Everything is just fine at home, they all send their regards, my wife too, and your brother Erich, of course. They all wish you'd come back to Switzerland one more time."

"There is no place like Switzerland," says the uncle.

The waitress brings coffee; the young lady pours for the uncle, adds milk and sugar, as much as he is allowed to have.

"You know that Alice has died," Peter says. "Erich wrote you about it."

"So they say," the uncle says. "Alice didn't die, she made herself die."

Peter, his eyes above the coffee cup, forgets to drink and for the length of a second he meets a malignant gaze which fades away immediately. Then the uncle digs out his watch again from under his sleeve. Peter swallows.

"At one time you wanted to become a surgeon, remember, Uncle?"

"So you know that," the uncle says calmly. "How could you know that? You know everything, don't you? But we couldn't make ends meet at home. And Mother—

that's something else. But Father. Father wanted us to bring home money right away. That's why——" The uncle is moving his lips a few times.

"You didn't have it easy, none of you," Peter says. "That's why you left, Alice and you, only Father stayed behind."

"Father was an unhappy human being," the uncle says. "He begrudged us every little bit of joy."

Peter does not set it right, he meant his own father, Erich; but the uncle knows only one father by now.

"You all went really far then," Peter says aloud and nods toward the uncle. "I was always proud of having an uncle in America whose visiting card read 'General Manager.' I think that's why I studied English. Besides, without you I couldn't have gone to the university."

"The walk to school was too long," the uncle says, "too long for children. One should keep that in mind. It shouldn't be that way. Father didn't pay enough attention to us. He didn't enjoy life either," the uncle said. Now the food arrives and the conversation is interrupted for a moment. Looking down at his plate with the steak on it the uncle says, "This looks good, looks very good." The uncle waits until the young lady's fish arrives, then he picks up his knife and fork. Once again he puts them both down. "This too looks very good," he says, bending over the young lady's fish and then, without transition, he looks into his lap. "The napkin is too small, perhaps. Should I now have a bigger napkin?"

"But you'll be careful, Mr. Shallenberger," the young lady says. "You know so well how to be careful now. Shall I cut up your steak?"

The uncle no longer listens. With his knife and fork he carefully begins to chisel off pieces of his steak, tiny pieces. One isn't sure if the meat is so tough the knife doesn't cut it, or if the uncle is afraid of making an uncontrollable move. He bends his head to meet each forkful, his face almost to the plate, and he swallows unobtrusively, as if the meat were stolen. This uncle had invited Peter to the first elegant meal of his life, an array of hors d'oeuvres which he was allowed to choose from a cart, after the uncle— much better than the waiter—had explained to him each individual dish; often the most unpretentious ones contained the true delicacies. The uncle knew this. He knew his way around in the world. Before the hors d'oeuvre, Peter was given a Pimm's Nr. 1, his first alcoholic beverage. That was in the airport restaurant, where they had international specialties. In those days in Dübendorf. And now he had invited his uncle for a tough steak.

The uncle points his fork at the steak. "This is exquisite, really exquisite."

"You don't get this every day at home, do you, Mr. Shallenberger," the lady with her drawling voice says across her fish which she has almost finished. "One is much better than the other," the uncle says carefully. Then a hint of embarrassment moves across his face and he bends over to the young lady. "I mean, one is good, but the other one is also good."

"It is also the right restaurant," the young lady says. "Not this silly luxury; instead, we feel perfectly at ease here, don't we."

A damn canteen, that's what it is, Peter is thinking, a feeding station with plastic flooring.

The uncle has pushed back his plate a little, the steak has been cut only around the edges, some french fries are missing and the mixed salad has not been touched.

"It was just right," the uncle says.

Peter swallows, but the lump of meat in his mouth remains unchanged, like wood. He is making a great effort to get it down so that he can talk. "They have fabulous desserts, Uncle," he says. "I saw them myself. Earlier, on the cart. About ten different kinds of pastry."

"Yes, that's just the thing for him," the young lady says, smiling. "But now you must indulge yourself a little. He never eats *more*," the young lady says, "not even at the home."

Peter beckons the pastry cart. The uncle gets a piece of fruit tart with a double portion of whipped cream, a bright green peppermint Jell-O, and two pieces of puff pastry. Now he eats very hastily, bending his head low over his plate as if he were lapping from it. At one point it seems to Peter that a drop has fallen onto the plate, maybe it was saliva. Once the uncle looks up and says, chewing, "I have never been here. Definitely not. I can't remember. Or were there other people? Were these people there?" he asks the young lady.

"Eat," she says digging into her ice cream. "Just eat in peace now." The uncle straightens up; the plate is empty. Then he bends down again to push a few crumbs on the fork. They keep falling off. He dabs them with a moist finger.

"It is great that you have such a nice garden at Cherokee Manor," Peter says. In earlier days the uncle had a well-tended garden around his house; it was blossoming in the first color photographs Peter had ever seen, and the uncle would also talk about it during his visits. When his wife was still living he spent every free minute in it.

"I am sure you often help, Uncle, in the garden at Cherokee Manor," Peter says.

"Beg your pardon?" the uncle asks and gives Peter a brief and sharp look. "Do I? I don't. What do you say?" he asks the young lady.

"Oh yes, he sometimes helps Mr. Bebee rake leaves and

with weeding, but the main thing for him is to see something green," says the young lady. It seems as if the uncle
wants to reply; then he presses his lips together.

"Would you also like an ice cream?" Peter asks. "You
must regain your strength."

The uncle scrutinizes him with hostility. "Yes, yes," he
says, "an ice cream." He continues very courteously.
"Everything has been just excellent. We are leaving now,"
the uncle says. "It is very pleasant here, isn't it."

Peter asks for the bill; the meal was inexpensive. He
pays at the cash register; the first moviegoers walk through
the adjacent vestibule. The uncle helps the young lady into
her light raincoat. He himself is not wearing a coat, just as
in the old days.

"You used to have a Studebaker, Uncle," Peter says,
opening the car door for them.

"Haha," the uncle says, "haha." He clears his throat.
This time he does not bump into anything.

They take another road back, described by the young
lady as scenic, passing harvested corn fields and dried up
sunflower stalks, through which a deep-colored lake
flashes, and white clapboard villages with classical portals.
The sun is barely visible as a red moon, the trees in their
fall foliage shine below a greenish sky like early evening
lights. The uncle has dozed off in the corner of the back
seat; he is not taking in anything. At every crossroad the
young lady directs Peter in whispers into a new part of the
country full of picturesque charms. The dried bloodstains
of the Sumac blossom above the withered roadside weeds,
overgrown, out of the semi-wilderness; a landscape for
Indians.

"He's so much better," says the young lady. "You
should have seen him three weeks ago, when he came to
us."

Finally the tires crunch on the gravel of the "hotel" esplanade; the uncle is awake. You can tell, because he breathes soundlessly, but he sits very quietly.

"Well, then," Peter says and helps them both out of the back of the rented car. The young lady says to the uncle, "In a minute you can have a real rest." They are standing outside the porch with its Doric capitals. Peter shakes hands with the young lady. Then he gives the uncle a wrapped gift package; a treat from back home. "Yes, he may have this," the young lady says. The uncle looks at his hands and the package. The young lady takes it away from him.

"One every night," she says. "We want it to last for a long time, don't we. Many thanks, say many thanks to Peter. It was such a lovely evening. Peter has come from so far to see you."

Peter lifts his arm toward his uncle's shoulder; then he feels himself drawn close. The uncle's bristly cheek presses against his cheek. The uncle's arm around Peter's shoulder squeezes and then Peter gets a hard kiss on each cheek. The uncle stays in Peter's arm a moment too long. But then Peter is left alone, and the young lady is leading the uncle, who can also walk by himself, toward the door. She pulls first the screen door, then the solid one and turns around to wave once more to Peter. But the uncle from America, as if he were still being led, his head slightly drawn in, walks into the house, which is actually nothing but a shack beneath too big a sky.

# THE COUNTRY HOUSE OR DEFAULTED PRESENCE

When I showed my face here for the first time she scolded
me terribly. At least that's the way I understood it. Whenever I approached the house—from whatever side—there
she was, outside her peeling door, or over there, in the
covered passageway, beginning to talk threateningly. It was
eerie: she always stood in the right spot, as if she had
nothing else to do but wait for me. The thought obsessed
me that not even at three A.M. could I have walked up to
this house, this group of old buildings, without someone
starting to talk in the dark. When I crossed the invisible
threshold of an area which perhaps coincided with a prior
claim or the playground of a grand-nephew long grown, I
released her voice, loosened sounds in a wrinkled throat at
which I looked only briefly and reluctantly while passing
by, a vehement but not overly loud protest, or what I
considered as such. Because the old woman could not be
understood. She let out a long stream of sounds clumsily

belabored by her tongue, yet her mouth didn't seem that of an old person, it even seemed to have a playful look if you brought yourself to observe closely.

I had been told that she was a deaf-mute, and indeed words of greeting, calls from a distance, had no effect on her, she would only scrutinize you with her strangely pale and restless eyes giving her face an expression of unsettling, almost malicious intelligence. Only when I reached a certain proximity to the house, would something begin to utter, almost chant from within her; I heard her singsong as a threat, felt exposed, as if I had had something wicked on my mind. When I walked past her and toward the house that I wanted to own, with a frozen smile, I suddenly felt like a trespasser sneaking around, and when I had them open the upper door leading to the part of the house that was for sale I heard the old woman raise her voice; it was as if I had hurt her by pressing down the door handle.

The owner, with whom I was dealing, led me around; he was a fairly young laborer who, almost blinded by an accident at the smelting furnace, had changed his mind about restoring and inhabiting the part of the house he had inherited, and he paid as little attention to the old woman as if she herself had been a piece of furniture, some sticks of wood or a wall. At the time there was no mention of her single room with its separate entrance being eventually for sale; she came up only incidentally in our talks, which were far from easy because of the local dialect. Harmless, that's what she was, living all by herself not hurting a soul; he had noticed the uneasiness she inspired in me and worried about my willingness to buy. As a matter of fact, the idea of living under the same roof with an old woman not quite right in her head did upset me, even if it were only for those few weeks during the year when I could get away from the office; to live here without any human contact or the possibility of it and yet within hearing of the old woman who, deaf and dumb or not, reacted so perceptibly. I wanted for myself a carefree environment where I would be allowed to remain a stranger without hurting anyone, and yet this woman who had lived in this spot seventy, perhaps eighty years had already been offended by my appearance.

This concern began to spoil my initial love for the house, which was historic but inconspicuous; except for the small part belonging to the old woman it had been vacant for many years, and from the empty and spacious room on the second floor which now contained nothing but a round soapstone stove bearing the date 1637, a calm had come over me which I called nostalgia. But the adjoining little room, where I had visualized my bed, five steps away from the stove and later from a desk, met wall to wall with the unknown domain of the old woman. And when — torn between my desire to find peace behind those enormous larchwood beams, in the unequivocal dimensions they established, and my uneasiness about the deaf-and-dumb neighbor — I had remained alone in this room for a few minutes, testing her silence, I heard something alive in the wall, a rustling and crackling which made me hold my breath. If it wasn't rats it was the old woman, and I fought unsuccessfully against the suspicion that if not now, some night, just there beyond the old wooden wall, she might start a fire.

My dreams stirred in opposition to my daytime fears whenever I inspected the house. At night in the nearby motel, where I had twice stayed thinking over the purchase of the house or at least my part of it, the old woman or some of her features appeared to me in the light of all-knowing kindness and I believe I pressed my head against the small-flower pattern of her dark smock and smelled

beneath it the odors of the Christmas manger and heard my
own heart beat like that of an unborn, firmly like a clock.

Her grand-nephew, who had turned up at my investigations together with other villagers (he too, by the way,
was an occupational invalid, who, thanks to a leg injury,
had returned to semi-idle peasant farming) accompanied
me to the house, talking to his great aunt when she
inevitably stepped into our path from the shadow of the
passageway where perhaps she had been staying for hours.
He demonstrated that one could talk to the woman and
claimed also to understand her. Although the voices—the
halfway intelligible speech of the grand-nephew, himself
no longer young, and the old woman's gurgling or drawling
utterances—alternated in a seemingly orderly way, I
didn't have the impression of an actual exchange. The
younger one seemed to pick up and report to me in some
form of High German only what he chose to hear: the aunt
was well, just now she had been resting, she was happy
because I had come. I considered every one of these
phrases untrue, not only because they obviously sprang
from a general courtesy and, further, from the nephew's
curiosity, but most of all because they actually *were*
phrases. If it was speech that the old woman was uttering,
it consisted not of phrases but of intonations, sung sound
groupings of her own invention which no one had yet
taken the trouble to decipher; clearly, after so much time,
she no longer expected such an effort. She no longer
listened to what the other would make of her message or
what was passed off as her message; she only watched its
effect on the unfamiliar face—mine—though so intensely
and with so much facial involvement that I doubted her
simple-mindedness, yes, even her disability. That she was
deaf and dumb all of a sudden seemed a convenient explanation for an unknown kind of human behavior, which

had isolated this woman, unmarried by the way, for many decades.

Nevertheless I provided my data as was proper: I was an attorney, with a Basel firm, in search of a second work-place which had to be quiet but not isolated; I no longer had a family; I was about to build myself a new life, and so on. In the meantime also the owner of the empty and much larger part of the house had turned up again. Despite his disability he moved quickly and eagerly, greeted the nephew and, after a pause, began to talk, in the presence of the old woman, about the burdens which could not be placed on her much longer. I gathered from this that he wanted to remind the nephew—obviously there had been a previous conversation—that I of course would be inter-ested in purchasing the entire house. The nephew nodded absentmindedly after a brief searching glance at my face, or, rather, at my mouth—people here never seemed to look into each other's eyes, only at the mouth. I must have nodded myself. Suddenly I felt petrified with shame because the eyes of the old woman were looking at me, fixedly and obviously fully aware of the situtation. I turned away, in order to examine the empty part of the house for the fourth or fifth time, accompanied by the two invalids who took turns leading the way.

The big room with the stove lay in its own light which seemed warmer and more familiar than the sunlight reflected in the finely articulated row of windows; the massive but not oppressive wooden walls breathed an ancient atmosphere which had remained undisturbed here. The last people who had lived in it, the family of a remote cousin, hadn't changed a thing, they hadn't had the money.

While we walked the seller repeated—perhaps to pre-vent any impression of his being overly business-minded and heartless—that the old woman, as long as she was still there, would hardly be of any trouble, and on her part could only be happy about a repaired roof. She was nowhere to be heard or seen now as we walked around the house, examining further annexes, all of them full of dusty and half-broken tools having to do with wine-growing and sheep-farming, which were to be included in the price of purchase, and odd antique pieces, chests, hand-forged tools, wine barrels, which the men promised not to claim for themselves if I had any use for them. They had no use for anything old, it seemed, and yet I observed with a great deal of embarrassment how the half-blind man, having already made his disclaimer, brought his face close to one such chest, trying to decipher the year and fingering the wood as though he had no rightful claim to his own things anyway, or as if for the first time he perceived himself, however listlessly, in the objects surrendered.

Only when we approached a stable, bolted by a small green padlock, did the old woman step again into our path—but no, she didn't—it was my own shock at her turning up forever unexpectedly which made me stop short. She had taken only one step from the respective dusk, but without stopping us, rather like someone acting on cue, reminding us of her existence but without any expectation that this would change anything. And she was right, because we busy men went past her.

On this occasion I cast a quick glance through the open door into her living quarters or their anteroom. Once again worn out things were crowded together, boxes with colored stickers, tin pitchers, a pile of coal briquettes, only here, even if the place wasn't tidy, there was no dust; surrounded by this junk somebody kept house and actually lived, although with difficulty. When we passed her in the narrow passageway she smoothed out her skirts, pressing her elbows to her sides. Opposite her entrance, in a lean-to of the stable, stood the outhouse, called a *gabiné* by the grinning nephew, that's how it was called here, and you smelled it too, the friable stench, not quite so raw any longer, of an old person.

The next day I approached the house only to bid it farewell. I parked at the waterfall whose quiet sound had once lured me and walked toward the property through wet weeds, wormwood almost as tall as myself. During the night the weather had changed; it was no longer raining, but the sky hung low in an un-summery way. Nothing stirred under the crumbling stone roofs which I would no longer have to repair. Nevertheless I walked the ground like a thief, prepared at every step to see the figure of the woman rise up. The cold haze also gave the village an uninhabited aspect, and my fingers clutched the key in my pocket as if it were a weapon. But this time there was not even a trace of the old woman.

In the middle of the passageway I stopped to look once more in peace at the handsome proportions of the cluster of roofs with their live cover in varying shades of gray, a perspective framed by the overhanging roof; so I would not live here after all. I visualized my own proprietary smoke rising from the chimney turret, whose modest Mediterranean design touched me. The next moment I stiffened, the right side of my face frozen with fear: close by, I didn't dare look, something huge had stirred. It was the deaf-mute woman; she was sitting in an old car seat among firewood—at one time it had been neatly stacked, but by now it had collapsed, through neglect, into a heap. She sat in her eternal dark skirts and the purplish-gray apron, her face framed by a kerchief of the same material, almost leaning back in repose, except for the upper part of her body, which was slightly raised. At the same time she lifted the fingers of one hand, lightly and without force, as if she had something to announce. I stared at her, trying to control my horror, and she followed the expression on my face with apprehension; when I felt the color return to my skin, her mouth slowly spread wide. I saw her upper and lower gums—no, she wasn't whimpering, her eyes sparkled. She was smiling, this had to be a smile. And then she spoke in cooing sounds which rose and fell while her lips tried to contain the smile. It became larger, began to move her whole face as she chattered on, involving not only the sunken cheeks but also the oddly smooth forehead. She nodded in my direction, not only with her head, but transformed her heavy body into a single beckoning gesture. The raised finger too, nodded, pointing to the house, her house. Only her eyes remained shining quietly, searching my face. I don't know how it happened: as a result of my tension I also formed sounds, in a language new to myself. For only a moment I felt inhibited: I might seem to be aping the invalid, mocking her. But there was no third person to notice and she herself did not take it in this way. Her eyes narrowed with pleasure when I interrupted her, her entire face showing signs of bliss and changing to an expression of encouragement; I had finally hit it right. She didn't listen to me, certainly not in the beginning. She continued to rattle, hum, click. She incited me not to slow down my babble. We croaked, scolded, grumbled, squeaked at each other, to any bystanders we would have sounded like a mad and childish duo, but there were just the two of us, the old woman and I, singing to each other between woodpiles at the back of the whole world.

Although I didn't understand every detail, on the whole it was now clear what she was telling me. That we were both alone, I and she, she and I, but we were no

longer alone at all. We would live together under that roof
there, and not only would we not be a nuisance to each
other we would have fun together — that's what she was
singing into my face, but not only that. Sometimes the
laboring in her face was stronger than her laughter, cut it
short, her eyes again opened wide, there was sorrow in
them, a child's fear, that I the newcomer, not wishing to
live there with her, would have it in his power to drive her
out. She implored me, and this I understood very well, not
to do it, please, to understand how cheerful she was, how
pleasantly one could live near her and that she wanted to
die there in her house, in our house. How it happened, I
don't know, but my voice, all by itself, took on a soothing
tone, turned into a coaxing cackle, I'd rather not call it a
lullaby. But she understood, wanted to grasp it, let her
voice die down, into mere whimpering sounds, sorrow
which could finally express itself, and contentment that
there was no longer any need for it. She wanted to believe
me, that I hadn't come from far away to drive her out with
my power, and so she fell silent now and then to take in the
voice which kept on soothing her and which was my own.

It was altogether inevitable: now I had to buy the
house, now I would buy with pleasure, and from now on
the old woman fell under my protection from everybody
else, as I, more mysteriously, fell under hers. The old
woman no longer made an effort to interrupt the flow of
her relief, to stop her throat and lips, to form what seemed
words and phrases. She drawled without stopping, swaying
backward and forward, to and fro, and I joined emphati-
cally in the strange vow. We had acquired a language in
which there wasn't a word left that one of us could have
broached. And when I finally took the key out of my
pocket, pointing to the house over there, and was about to
leave, and yes, I bowed, I saw her nod, the tears gushing

from her eyes, and she no longer took her folded hands from her lap to wipe them off. And I went over to her, before I could turn away, and squeezed those two hands of hers, let her once more grasp everything, held on when the snot dripped down on the back of my hand.

That afternoon I drove into town with the half-blind man to settle the deal, to have the papers drawn up which in the valley are called "the act." When the seller pointed out to me that the old woman's property would become available in the near future, after all she was almost ninety, and couldn't go on much longer, I objected sharply. He confirmed that she was harmless, even if children were afraid of her and, for that reason, played nasty tricks on her. She was the only one of her generation who had remained in the parents' house, her siblings had either disappeared overseas or moved to "outer Switzerland," many to die young, like most people. How many of them had there been? Ten, he believed, or eleven. They had all lived in that part of the house, yes, thirteen people in one room, but there was also the kitchen where the children had slept and it had been warmer too. Now the old woman was alone, with plenty of room, they had let her live there as long as she could manage; that part of the house, those two rooms, were only one sixth or one seventh her own, that's how ownership was in the valley, had always been this way as far as he knew. But the rest of the family for the time being did not claim its part, having bettered themselves in the meantime, "made it," the man said. They didn't bother about the old aunt, only the grand-nephew whom I had met and two married nieces had stayed in the neighborhood. That was the advantage of large families, he said, it was always somebody's lot to take care of the old so they wouldn't be altogether lost, and religion saw to that, too.

The invalid was sorry to hear that I would only be able to return in the late fall, since I had some important trials up until that time; so I was an attorney; the blind man had already guessed it, he said, when he had heard me talk to the lawyer. That I was an expert and read books, one could hear very well. It was an honor for the village that a stranger like myself wanted to vacation, almost to live here, later on one could exchange one or the other service. Late fall was generally a very dry period here, and repairs could be done more easily in winter when there was no farm work, trades were also slack, alas, and in the village there would be scarcely anybody who wouldn't like to lend me a hand after work for extra money. It must be a good feeling to have the house "put to one side" in the meantime; it wasn't exactly comfortable but for connoisseurs like myself quite a find. If it hadn't been so difficult, on account of his eyes, he would have kept it himself and now he was wishing me good luck with it.

When I returned in the later part of October, I first parked at the waterfall, which rushed more strongly than during the summer, looked at my house from afar, relished it, approaching it slowly, every step through the worm-wood, now sparse, saw the roof shine gray and peaceful through the discolored bushes. In the passageway sat the car seat, covered with dust, between the woodpiles. The house gave no sign of life, all the shutters, even the old woman's light green ones, were closed. Something like caution prevented me from entering; I walked around the house to check and then decided to look up first its former owner, the young invalid. On the short stretch the nephew joined me; somewhere he seemed to have waited for me. Did she die? I asked him. — No, but she is doing well, he said. We put her into the home for the elderly, there was a vacancy. — But why? I asked and stopped. — It wouldn't have worked out for much longer, he said. And when you bought the other part of the house there was no room left for the aunt. —Who said so? I asked sharply. —But you want the house in its entirety, he said, or else you can't really do much with it. Now you're getting it for a decent price. I have talked it over with the relatives, it's yours for six thousand including the basement, where you can put your bathroom now.—

Indeed, that's what I had said on the first day, when I hadn't yet understood the situation, when I hadn't promised anything yet to the old woman. —That had been meant for later on, you must know, not at any price did I want to drive out your aunt. —But there was a vacancy in the home, he said, that doesn't happen every day, it was an opportunity and she even sees some of the money. We already cleared out her apartment. —I looked at him, dismayed; he remained calm and was quite certain that he had interpreted my desire for unencumbered property correctly and took my shock for mere formality. —And what did she have to say to this? I asked softly. —Her legal guardian approved, he said. We took her for a little ride (I learned that he had bought a car), had a cup of coffee with her along the road and then we left her there. —She is doing well, he said, she is in a room of four where she no longer has to look after her own heating, gets her food every day and we don't have to be afraid that she might get hurt or get into some mischief. —That's not what I wanted, I said. I walked on slowly; he followed me.

It is not your concern, he said. We were the ones who had to look after her, and my wife has bad legs, it was becoming too much. —How do you know that she likes being there? I asked. —We talked to her, he said. True, she still thinks she'll be able to come back some day, but that won't be possible.

He was a quiet man, he didn't stop walking when he talked, but he didn't look at me as I looked at him, he didn't have a bad conscience; only when he talked of the aunt's belief in her eventual return he gave me a look in which a suggestion of emphasis or reproach could be read; but not a reproach aimed at anyone in particular, rather at the way of the world and its daily decline, which nobody could help, least of all someone from this village.—Something might have happened, he said, and you would not always have been there, nor would we. She's not dangerous, he said, but she doesn't always know what she is doing, and the heating had become a problem, the wife had seen to it for the past two winters but her legs aren't getting any better. "The wife" was his wife.

He himself dragged one leg as he was saying this, walking was a strain on him, although we didn't hurry; why should we have been in a hurry, and where was I going anyhow. Only one thing was certain: someone who didn't belong here, who came from the outside and left whenever it suited him, had no other humanity to bring here. He was a fancier of old stone roofs and stoves with a date on them and when he wanted to be humane he adjusted his bid accordingly.

—She is doing well, the nephew said once more.

I bought the old woman's part of the house, at a price which was more than acceptable to the dispersed family. Remodeling cost me a good deal more than planned. There was no longer any good reason for not building at least a bathroom with the usual comfort in the old woman's basement. The roof had to be tiled anew, with greenish tiles, since the gray stone is no longer being quarried and collecting undamaged tiles from demolished dwellings would have been too expensive. As for the rest of the house, I have left it as it was, including the old woman's room. It is the only room in the house which is not in style, ugly if you like. To protect it against extreme cold, some-one had nailed varnished hard-wood paneling over the larchwood beams and put in a small wood stove. In October it had already been cleared of the ashes and the nephew had taken over the old woman's few pieces of furniture himself, cutting some into firewood and throwing them outside on the wood carrier; a special service for me because coal heat is too much for my seventeenth-century stove. The ceiling in the room where a family of twelve or thirteen once lived is painted over with zinc green as in other rural areas. I put in a tubular steel bed and called it a guest room; actually I don't use it and rarely even enter it. A few blackened rags which she must have stuck in from the outside between door frame and wall to ward off the draught still remind me of its last occupant. On the oppo-site wall hangs a Magritte poster; the well-known tree with the door in the stem opening onto a faraway house well-lit at night. The little iron stove which used to stand there has been ditched into the brook, not far below the waterfall, by the nephew or someone else; it can't pollute and regula-tions concerning the maintenance of embankments and things of that sort are not strict in these parts. Therefore my house now appears in its dark stain and with its shiny row of windows and the heavy stone roof as the only dwelling of its period in the village worthy of preservation.